HOMESPUN HARVEST

HOME TO  HEATHER CREEK™

HOMESPUN HARVEST

Robert Elmer

Guideposts
NEW YORK, NEW YORK

Home to Heather Creek is a trademark of Guideposts.

www.guideposts.com
(800) 431-2344
Guideposts Books & Inspirational Media

Cover by Lookout Design, Inc.
Interior design by Cindy LaBreacht
Typeset by Nancy Tardi
Printed in the United States of America

Acknowledgments

My Danish grandmothers, who never ran out of hugs or cookies, had a deep and abiding influence on my life. This story is dedicated to them and to all the other wonderful grandmothers who make such a difference in the lives of their grandchildren. Perhaps you're one of them! As someone once said, a grandmother is a mother who has a second chance.

—Robert Elmer

Chapter One

"Uh-oh."

Even from ten feet away, Charlotte could see poor little Christopher's face turn as red as Amanda Hotstetler's strawberry Jell-O supreme when his cup of fruit punch spilled all over the potluck serving table. Janie Richmond's scalloped potatoes were the first victim, though Charlotte had to admit a little punch probably wouldn't hurt them to any large degree. Even so, she grabbed a handful of napkins from the stack at the end of the table and flew to her grandson.

"Don't worry, Christopher." She mopped at the punch furiously before it had a chance to cascade over the edge of the red-checkered plastic tablecloth. "No harm done."

Christopher didn't look so sure, and he backed up with his plate as if he had completely ruined the annual All Saints Harvest Potluck, which he had not.

"I-I'm sorry, Grandma," he stammered. "It just slipped."

"Smooth move, Superman." Christopher's older brother Sam came up behind him in the potluck line, balancing a Chinet plate in his left hand and playfully punching his little brother in the shoulder with his right. "Couldn't have done better myself."

"Sam!" Charlotte chased the drips under the plate of honey-sliced ham DeeDee Meyers had proudly displayed in the middle of the table. Around it, a green bean casserole had escaped significant damage, along with a dish of pork and beans topped with crumbled bacon and onions. "It could have happened to anybody. And there, see?"

She swiped the table for good measure, just to show them it was nothing to get upset about.

"Oooh!" Nancy Evans, the pastor's wife, leaned over the table from the other side, smiling and waving with her hand as if to waft a little more of the aromas her way. To her credit, she had overlooked the spilled punch, acting as if nothing had happened. "Everything smells sooo good here, doesn't it?"

Charlotte had to admit, the ladies of the Bedford Community Church Hospitality Committee had outdone themselves this time. Although the Harvest Potluck usually brought out the best in Bedford's cooks each year, Charlotte wasn't sure what had gotten into them this year. Maybe they'd all been inspired by the latest cooking-show craze some of the other ladies had mentioned—a perky young New Yorker who traveled the country doing home-spun cooking demonstrations. She would be coming to the fairgrounds for a taping in a few days. Charlotte couldn't remember the name, something like Constance or Courtney. Something with a C.

Most of the recipes that she'd heard of from the cooking

show seemed far too rich for her family's tastes. Bob would never touch something like a tuna and mango sashimi salad or provolone risotto with cherry tomatoes, even if she had been able to find the ingredients at Herko's Grocery Store.

Even so, the tables for the All Saints event did look lovely, if she said so herself. As her grandchildren moved back into the line she stood back to admire their work. Each of the four serving tables featured a different centerpiece.

Jerri Smithgall's table featured a wonderful cornucopia of dried yellow squash, Indian corn, and bright orange pumpkins.

Arlis Bauer's table used leftover candy bars from the previous day's trick-or-treating, built into the shape of . . . perhaps a Pilgrim's hat? To be honest, Charlotte couldn't be quite sure, and she wasn't about to ask.

Though the fourth table was supposed to be visited last, already a sizable crowd had gathered around the side where Charlotte had set up her cherry-berry and apple-caramel pies.

"Save some for me!" Rick Bauer, Arlis's husband, headed into the fray. Obviously he would not be denied a slice. Arlis had to turn sideways to work through the crowd with a refill of cream for the coffee.

"It's the same every year, Char!" She looked over at Charlotte with a big smile. "Makes me think we should call out the sheriff, just so there isn't a riot around your pies."

Charlotte smiled inwardly at the compliment, even as she felt a little guilty for doing so. They were just her mother-in-law Mildred's recipes, after all. Though she had to admit, Mildred had baked the best pies in Adams County, perhaps in all of Nebraska.

She turned back to see how her three grandchildren were managing as they shuffled past the third table.

Christopher seemed to have recovered well enough, as ten-year-olds do as a matter of course. A shy smile had replaced his earlier embarrassment as he held out his plate for her to see.

"Somebody made enchiladas," he told her, pointing at his prize. "See?"

Sam came up right behind him and grunted his disapproval.

"Not as good as we used to get at Ortega's," he said, wrinkling his nose. "Back *home.*"

He emphasized the last word as he pushed past with his own plate, and his tone should not have surprised Charlotte. Even after several months of living with their grandparents at Heather Creek Farm, Sam still seemed to keep one foot back in San Diego. No matter how much Charlotte reached out to the wounded little birds, Sam and his two younger siblings still guarded their hearts well. Sam took every chance he could to remind them of what they had left behind when their mother died late last spring.

Time, Charlotte, she reminded herself. *Give them more time.*

Only, how much more did they have with a sixteen-year-old who just wanted to go back to California, a fourteen-year-old going on twenty-two, and a ten-year-old who still didn't seem to have a friend in the world?

At this rate, how long before she and Bob found their hearts broken once again by another good-bye note left on their pillow? Would they ever find a way into their grandchildren's hearts, wounded so deeply by their mother's death?

Certainly they had introduced the kids to farm chores, and Bob always made sure they read the Scriptures together after every dinner. They'd done everything they knew to do, including faithfully bringing them to church every week and to events like this annual potluck.

Charlotte couldn't help recalling once again the verse in Proverbs about training up a child in the way he should go. But would Christopher, Sam, and Emily ever really understand what their grandparents valued the most, or what they really lived for? Charlotte glanced up at the clock on the wall of the basement fellowship hall, all too aware of the early darkness and the approaching winter. November 1 already, and the sun had set by 5:20 PM. But winter wasn't the only approaching darkness.

"Excuse me, Grandma." Emily approached with a plate of pasta salad and greens, though she'd only eaten a bowl of granola and a banana for breakfast. Maybe she didn't think her grandmother was keeping track.

"Why don't you try some of that casserole?" Charlotte suggested, anticipating Emily's reaction. "I think it has little chunks of broccoli in it."

Christopher stood nearby, wolfing down another bite as he edged a little closer. Charlotte wished he would find a place to sit down, rather than risk dumping his plate on the floor.

"You've got to be kidding, Grandma." Emily made a face, as if Charlotte had said something truly absurd. "Do you have any idea how much saturated fat is in a cheese-and-grease special like that?"

Charlotte grimaced at Emily's description of Nancy Evans' best efforts. She brought a finger to her lips as a reminder, but too late.

"Probably a hundred grams per serving." Emily pointed straight at Christopher's plate. "Do you want to die of a heart attack at age twelve?"

Christopher paused with his fork in midair, still chewing his "cheese and grease," before glancing from Charlotte to his sister with a look of puzzlement. Emily didn't seem to catch the directed frown from Charlotte, who was clearly signaling her to cease and desist.

"I thought it tasted pretty good." Christopher swallowed his next bite with some effort, as if the casserole had suddenly solidified. "And aren't heart attacks just for old people?"

"No, they're not." Emily was on a roll, and her voice carried way too far as she set her plate to the side. "I was reading that almost twenty percent of American kids are way obese, and it's because of junk like that. I couldn't eat something like that."

"Emily, that's quite enough." By this time, despite her best efforts to appear cool and casual, Charlotte's ire began to bleed through in the serious tone of her voice and the tense set of her jaw. She was also painfully aware of sideways glances from other members of the church Hospitality Committee as they passed by. She finally lowered her voice in an attempt to shush her granddaughter.

"We don't say those kinds of things about food that others have spent a lot of time preparing."

"Well, I wouldn't eat it, Grandma." With her hands parked firmly on her hips, Emily wasn't backing down that easily. "I just wouldn't."

"No one's making you eat it. But if you don't have anything good to say, please don't—"

A crash behind her made Charlotte whirl, but it wasn't a child this time. Nancy Evans stood facing them with a stricken look on her face and a Corelle plate twirling at her feet. She immediately crouched to scoop it up, mumbling something about "butterfingers."

But there was no pretending the damage hadn't already been done. The pastor's wife had undoubtedly heard Emily's every unkind word, and Charlotte knew she could not let it pass. Not this time. So almost before Nancy had straightened back up with her plate, Charlotte touched Nancy's shoulder and steered Emily out of the supper line, taking them both aside. Emily acted as if she had no idea how far she'd just placed her foot in her mouth.

"Please, Nancy." Charlotte took a deep breath. "You have to excuse her for speaking out like that about your casserole. I'm sure she didn't— I mean, Denise has to learn that we just don't—"

"No, Charlotte, it's quite all right." Nancy obviously

tried to shake it off as she gained back her composure. "We don't all have to like the same things."

This time, though, it was Emily's turn to flush, and Charlotte kept her from turning aside with a firm grip on her arm. Her eyes started to fill with tears, and Charlotte could have kicked herself for forcing this confrontation. Even in the comparatively quiet corner of the basement, she hadn't expected quite this much of a reaction from her granddaughter.

"You called me Denise," Emily whispered, wiping away the tears with the back of her hand and setting her plate of salad down on a nearby table.

"I . . . what?" Charlotte released her grip. What had started as an awkward moment was now turning into something far worse.

"You called me Denise." Emily repeated herself quietly, but the tears still welled in her eyes as she looked at them both. "Look, I'm sorry for being rude, Mrs. Evans. I didn't know it was such a big deal. But, Grandma, I'm not my mother, and you can't treat me the same way you did her."

Without another word Emily ran for the back door to the parking lot, ignoring quizzical looks from her brothers. Charlotte bit her lip, fighting the feeling that she had just stepped back in time, back to when she and Denise had argued about the length of her skirt on the night of the Bedford High School junior prom.

"Did I really call her that?" Charlotte whispered, and Nancy rested a hand on her shoulder. In the twelve years the pastor and his wife had served Bedford Community

Church, Charlotte couldn't remember a time when she'd come face-to-face with the kind of situation that made her wish she could just crawl away and hide.

She supposed there was a first time for everything.

"I know it's been hard for you," Nancy told her. "And I'm so sorry I reacted like that. If I'd been thinking, I would have just ignored it. Really. I should have. I'm sorry."

"You're not the one who should be apologizing. But thank you for being so sweet about it." By this time Charlotte had worked up to being good and mad at herself. For forcing the issue in public. For crushing her granddaughter's spirit. She squeezed Nancy's hand and stepped away. "I'd better go see if I can make repairs."

Only, how? She had no idea as she hurried after Emily, out into the darkness of the November evening. Behind her, a golden glow escaped the church windows to flicker across the parking lot behind the building and the grove of maples that flanked the church.

This time of year, bare branches pointed accusing fingers at her as they swayed in the cold wind. She shivered and hugged her shoulders more tightly, wishing for a coat, before stepping past a frosted lineup of pickup trucks, away from the weakening radius of church light and closer to the little picnic area.

The youth group had dug a fire pit there years ago, back when Denise had been involved. Had it really been all that long ago? If the leaded night sky had not been threatening to let loose more sleet, they might have even enjoyed a bonfire there tonight.

Now, though, the grove only hid shadows of memories,

and, she prayed, perhaps her heartbroken granddaughter.

Please, Lord, she whispered the prayer as she shuffled closer, *I need to find her.*

And then what would she do? As her eyes adjusted to the dark she thought she saw a shadow pull back behind one of the larger trees.

"Emily?" She gathered all her courage and stepped into the grove. Unfortunately the toe of her shoe caught an unseen snag, sending her stumbling for balance. Her frightened yelp must have flushed Emily from her hiding place. A moment later Charlotte felt a hand on her arm, helping her to her feet.

"I'm pretty clumsy, aren't I?" Charlotte ventured. "In more ways than one."

"You okay?" Emily sounded concerned. When Charlotte looked over at her granddaughter, she could barely make out her face in the faint light. She looked so much like Denise.

"Look, Emily, I'm so sorry for what I said back there. You know it was just a slip of the tongue. I just wanted you to know that what we say can hurt people, without our meaning to. And then, just to illustrate the point, I went and did the same thing, didn't I?"

She waited a minute, wondering if Emily would run off and leave her alone in the picnic grove again. She tried to hold Emily's hand, but Emily pulled away.

"I'm sorry for shooting off my mouth, Grandma." Emily's voice still trembled, though it could have been from the chill wind that now cut through them. Neither wore a sweater. "And I'm sorry that . . . the casserole was so gross."

This time Charlotte let it slide. Emily had something else to say, and her voice shook.

"But, Grandma—"

"It's not about the food, is it?" Charlotte knew, even if Emily couldn't admit it. "Are you still sad about your friend Rayann moving away? At least you and Ashley seemed to have patched up your friendship, right?"

Sure enough, Emily didn't answer, and Charlotte dug deep for a way to ease the tense standoff or to connect somehow with her granddaughter.

"You know, holidays always make me think of my father." Charlotte finally sighed and went on, braving the silence. "Your great-grandfather. Every year, he would go out hunting with a couple of my uncles, and they would come back with a Thanksgiving pheasant. Two, if they were lucky. Then my mother would fix it up just like you would think a turkey would be, with spices that made our little house smell good for days, and a wonderful stuffing. I always kicked myself for never getting the recipe, though. You might have liked it."

"A bird? That's totally gross."

"Gross? You know we eat chicken all the time. And turkey."

"*You* do."

"Better than a cheese-and-grease special."

Emily actually giggled at that and finally allowed her grandmother to slip an arm gently around her shoulder.

"We should go back in," Charlotte told her, "before we both turn into Popsicles."

"Or another tornado hits."

As she shivered once more, Charlotte was afraid her granddaughter's wounds were much deeper than she'd feared.

And she had no idea how to make them better.

Chapter Two

What do you think of this, Grandma?"

Christopher's face looked hopeful as he handed up the brightly colored Sears wishbook that had come in the mail the day before, just before they'd left for the church potluck. With page after page of toys, it didn't surprise her that he had commandeered the catalog first. Charlotte paused from her Sunday afternoon dishes, wiped soapsuds on her apron, and took the catalog from his hand. He tapped one of the pages.

"It's the new Nintendo system," he told her. "Everybody has it, except us."

"Everybody?" She arched her eyebrows and then squinted to make out the print on the catalog page, most of which was intended for people with eyes much younger than her own.

"Well, everybody back in San Diego," he admitted, grabbing back the catalog and flipping a couple of well-worn pages forward. "They had it last year. Mom said we couldn't afford it. But I found something else. What about this?"

This time she studied the page where he pointed out a full-featured, wireless weather station, complete with a wind tracker, a digital readout, and a computer interface.

"It says it's just like they use on the Weather Channel," Christopher said quickly. "I could set it up out by the barn, and then I could tell you all the latest weather reports myself."

"Very ambitious of you, Christopher." She dabbed a bit of suds on his nose, which he promptly shook off. "But the price is pretty ambitious too. I don't suppose you noticed that?"

She pointed, wishing it weren't so.

"One forty-nine ninety-nine." He read the price carefully. "Plus shipping and handling. That's not so much. Is it?"

"I wish it wasn't. But I'm afraid that's more than we can afford for Christmas, dear. We'll find something a little less, you know, expensive."

Or a *lot* less expensive. For a moment Charlotte actually did the mental math, adding up what it would take to buy each of the grandkids something special this Christmas—their first Christmas at the farm, without their mother, away from their home in California. Surely she and Bob could scrape together a little extra to make it special for them.

Couldn't they?

She dunked her hands once again in the hot, sudsy water and snapped back to reality. Not for $149.99. Not for half that. Her grocery budget this time of year was slim enough already, especially with the three extra mouths to feed, and school clothes, shoes and winter coats to buy.

But how could they explain that to an eager-eyed young man who just wanted a weather station for Christmas? Christopher retreated to the breakfast nook and plopped his catalog down on the well-worn oak kitchen table with a sigh, and then reached down to scratch his brown tabby, Lightning, behind the ears. Charlotte did her best to soften the blow.

"It's not that we wouldn't love to get you a nice gift," she said softly, staring at the bare yard outside her kitchen window. A lone goldfinch, still in its bright yellow summer plumage, picked at the feeder Bob had built for her last year. Finding nothing, it disappeared again into the gray gloom. She made a mental note to have Bob refill the feeder right away.

"But even if we can't," she went on, "you know that we're going to have a wonderful Thanksgiving together. That comes first. No need to rush things the way they do in the stores, right? Christmas will come soon enough. You wait and see."

"Sure." What else could Christopher say? He sat at the table, absently flipping pages with Lightning on his lap as Charlotte scrubbed at a stubborn fry pan that had begun to lose its nonstick surface. A new pan would probably be on her list. She wondered if all the little black specks in that morning's scrambled eggs had not been pepper.

I don't need any expensive gifts, she told the Lord as she inspected the pan before placing it on the drying rack. *But the children?*

The Lord didn't answer, but out in the family room, she heard a whoop as her three men enjoyed the football game on television. By the sound of things, someone must have just made a good play, though the cry hadn't been quite loud enough to signal a touchdown.

She couldn't complain. If nothing else, at least college football could bring her elder and younger sons into the same room as their father. On a Sunday afternoon like today she would gladly grant them a three-hour reprieve from the day's chores.

"Where's Sam?" she asked Christopher, hanging up her dish towel. "Do you think he'd want to watch the game with Grandpa and the uncles?"

Christopher shrugged. "Dunno. Sam still says football is lame."

Sam had been a kicker on the high school team this fall, but he never seemed to warm to the sport. "Not as much action as soccer," Christopher said.

Charlotte smiled. "Well, he'd better not say so in public, especially around Uncle Pete."

"Or what?" Christopher looked up at her with a genuine question.

"I'm just teasing," she told him. The TV's volume seemed to go down during a commercial. "But you know how people get about college football around here. It's a very big deal in this part of the country."

"I guess so." He buried his nose back in the catalog as she busied herself replacing dishes in the cupboard. From out in the family room the voice of her elder son, Bill, seemed to turn especially serious. Despite herself, her ears perked up.

"I know you're not worried right now, Dad," said Bill. "I'm sure Pete's a good help to you."

"Darn right," Pete chimed in. "With corn prices coming up a little this year, we broke even. Can't everybody say that. So we're doing okay."

Bill raised his voice. "See, but that's exactly my point." Charlotte frowned, but Christopher still had his nose in the catalog and didn't seem to notice. "Everybody thought the Millers were running a tight operation too, and look what happened to them. I've been thinking—"

So that's what this is about. Charlotte hadn't been sure if Bill's after-church visit without his family was just to come watch the game with his father and brother. She looked around for a sponge to wipe down the table, though she'd already done it once.

"Christopher, you think Stormy needs someone to check on her out in the barn?" Charlotte motioned toward the door. "You can take a carrot to feed her."

"No thanks." Christopher shook his head and lifted his catalog out of the way, so she could get at the table. "Emily takes care of the horses. And it's too cold."

He seemed content sitting right where he was, turning the pages of his catalog and eavesdropping on the men. She thought of simply shooing him out as Bill launched into his pitch once more, but in fact it *was* pretty chilly outside.

"Look," Charlotte heard Bill continuing, "I know neither of you wants to think about this kind of thing, just like Mom and Dad don't want to think about updating their will and designating guardians for—"

"Let's not start with that guardian stuff again," Pete broke in.

"All right, all right." Bill seemed to retreat. "But you can't tell me you've been making enough in the past five years to actually keep ahead. You have to make profits to stay in business, not just break even."

"We're doing okay, Bill." That was Bob's line. They were always doing okay.

"You say that, but I'm afraid it's actually starting to get away from you. Keeping it together with baling wire and bubble gum, right?"

Christopher wrinkled his nose in confusion at Uncle Bill's comment about gum, but Charlotte didn't care to explain right now. Instead she held a finger to her lips, in case he was thinking of asking, as Bill went on.

"And I know the last thing you want to do is sell out to one of those agribusiness conglomerates, like the Millers did, but—"

"The Millers," put in Bob, "and before that, the Westmorlands. But that was last year. Things are a little better this year."

"I know, Dad. But the point is . . ." By this time Charlotte could see her elder son pacing around the family room the way he did when he was in campaign mode. He'd done the same thing when he was running for mayor of River Bend. He stopped with his back to the kitchen and planted his hands on his hips.

"The point is," said Bill, "the Millers sold out, but they got top dollar for their land."

"So?" Pete obviously still wasn't convinced.

"You still don't see?" Bill resumed his pacing. "Okay, then. Look at it this way. It's just like that wide receiver for the Huskers. What's his name, Blake?"

"You mean Jamal Blaine," Pete corrected him.

"You know who I'm talking about. The guy got injured, but he kept it quiet and they kept him in the lineup, like he was some kind of tough guy."

"I thought he was tough," said Pete.

"But then he tried to play, and now he's made it all worse, and it looks like his chances for playing pro ball are down the tubes."

"I don't see what that's got to do with us," countered Pete. "This ain't no ball game, and we're not injured."

"Not yet. But if you look at what you could do with the money now, I mean, it opens up a whole new level. Instead of being behind all the time, you could be ahead. You could actually invest in something that will provide for Mom and Dad in a couple of years."

"I'm not out to pasture just yet, Bill," objected Bob.

"Dad! If you wait until something really bad happens, then it's too late. There's a company buying *now*. They're looking for property in this area to consolidate their holdings. You go out on top of your game."

"That's about the dumbest thing I've ever heard." Pete could be rather blunt when he wanted to be.

Bob grunted at that, too, and the game snapped back on as someone other than Bill obviously grew impatient with the course of this conversation.

"All I'm saying . . ." Bill raised his voice above the game announcer's. Charlotte heard a pep band in the background blasting out one of their favorite University of Nebraska fight songs, "There Is No Place Like Nebraska." From the sound of things, the crowd was enjoying the moment, with plenty of stomping and cheering. But Bill would have none of it.

"Pete, would you turn that thing down for just a second?"

Another grunt as the crowd noise abated by a few decibels. "I thought you came here to watch the game," complained Pete, "not give us financial advice."

"All I'm saying is, give it some serious thought. Before it's too late and we lose the whole place, okay? I think we have an opportunity right now that we should consider seriously."

"We?" Pete's voice went up a notch.

"You! We! Whatever!" Now Bill's voice could be heard easily throughout the house. "I'm just trying to tell you there's an open door right now, and it's not going to be open very long. You understand what I'm saying?"

He got no reply that Charlotte could hear, though she could imagine Bob and Pete's icy looks. And by this time she wished she had shooed Christopher outside while she'd still had the chance. The boy didn't need to hear adults arguing like this about things like this.

Just then Bill came storming through the kitchen, yanking his jacket on as he went. Christopher followed every move with wide eyes.

"Bye, Mom," Bill said. "I've got to go. It's getting thick in there."

She opened her mouth to say something but changed her mind. He left her with a peck on the cheek, and a blast of cold air rustled her yellow-checked curtains before the back door slammed just a little more loudly than she would have liked.

In the family room, the football game returned to full volume and then some. And there in the kitchen, Christopher's surprised expression hadn't quite returned to normal.

"Are they really going to sell the farm?" he asked, his voice low. He'd obviously heard enough to get the gist of the argument. Even a ten-year-old would have to be deaf not to.

"No, honey." She tried her best to reassure him. "That was just your Uncle Bill talking, and you know how he's always coming up with new ideas. Of course your grandfather would never sell this place."

"You sure?"

"Scout's honor."

As she turned to look out the kitchen window again, the cold November clouds let loose with another load of sleet, pummeling what was left of her garden. At the same time Bill kicked up gravel with his silver Toyota sedan as he headed back out to Heather Creek Road, his lights picking their way past the long row of windbreak elms that seemed to lose themselves in the midafternoon gloom.

Bob's father had planted those trees after a wicked ice storm took out most of the original elms from a generation earlier. She remembered that storm as a young teenager, hardly older than Christopher, when power in Bedford was out for over a week. Hadn't it started out with sleet that time as well?

She shook her head. It had been too long ago, but hardly any time at all since a dark-haired Bob Stevenson first brought her to this place. She did remember how he'd insisted on taking her on a "tour" of the farm, explaining all about who had built each building and when. Bob's great-grandfather Albert had built the barn and the beginnings of the main house, the oldest buildings on the farm. Subsequent generations had added on or rebuilt several portions, adding their own touches. Five generations of Stevensons—no, six—had lived here.

Even so, Charlotte preferred the more personal reminders of their past, like the little heart-shaped stepping-stone Pete had made her for a Sunday school project when he was eleven. The black pebbles that had once spelled out "Jesus Loves My Mom" had long since fallen out, but the stepping-stone remained in a place of honor just below her kitchen window, near the back door. Today, the stone lay hidden under a carpet of elm leaves and slush. She wished she could see it now.

And still she wondered: Was there a chance Bill could be right? What would it take for them to sell the farm, like the Millers and the Westmorlands? Certainly the money would come in handy, both now and for the future. In a few years Sam would want to go to college—not to mention Emily and Christopher. As of today, they had no way of providing that opportunity, unless God stepped up with a miracle and opened the doors. And what about the Christmas to come?

"Maybe it's a good thing you didn't go outside, Christopher." She finally let go the memories, for now. "It's looking pretty bleak out."

But when she turned back around, she realized she'd only been talking to herself. Christopher had disappeared with Lightning, leaving his catalog open to the page with the weather forecasting station.

One hundred forty-nine dollars, she thought, *and ninety-nine cents.*

Chapter Three

The next evening Charlotte pulled her scarf a little more tightly around her neck, wondering why she had ever let her friend Hannah talk her into coming out on a dreary night like this. She nearly slipped again on the icy sidewalk leading to the Adams County Fairgrounds while the tall, long-striding Hannah led the way through the crowds of women all headed the same direction. She waved their pair of tickets back at Charlotte from the entry turnstiles.

"Come on, girl!" She motioned impatiently. "We want to get a good seat, don't we?"

Well, that would be fine. Once they entered the large green exhibition hall, Hannah dragged her all the way to the front, past DeeDee and Arlis from church and right up next to Melody, whose bright, round face lit up when she saw them.

"I knew you two would come." Melody looked around at the barn, which during fair times housed everything from 4-H displays to hot tubs and candy-corn sellers. Tonight it looked nothing like they might have expected, but was no less full of people and activity. Along the back wall, roll-down covers masked three unused serving windows from the Fair Grill, normally operated by the Bedford Schools PTA. Charlotte had put in her share of hours in that kitchen years ago.

Tonight, though, the sizable room was filled with several sets of bleachers, all facing a stage festooned with autumn decorations like cornstalks and gourds, and flanked by lights on tall stands and a pair of TV cameras on tripods. Two big-screen monitors had been mounted to stands on either side of the grand centerpiece—a large demonstration kitchen counter, at least twenty feet wide and equipped with every known kitchen gadget. A mirror as big as the flag above the Adams County Courthouse had been hung at an angle above the center counter, to give the audience a bird's-eye view of what their celebrity chef was going to prepare for them.

Melody, a well-fed, always-smiling woman in her mid-forties, leaned over to speak above the noise of the crowd.

"I can't believe Cindi Slate would come here to Bedford." Her voice bubbled with excitement. "Can you?"

In a crowd like this, Charlotte wasn't about to admit she wasn't a faithful watcher of Miss Slate's popular cooking show, but she knew her friends watched the program religiously, and she smiled politely in return.

"I suppose it's . . . pretty unusual."

"I heard they might make tonight part of her show." Melody adjusted her bright aqua and orange scarf. "And that she's been having demonstrations like this in small towns all over Nebraska. You know the part on the show where they visit little restaurants and kitchens, and interview the cooks?"

"What if they came to Mel's Place?" Hannah put in from Charlotte's left side. Melody responded with a nervous giggle. Nothing like a national TV celebrity to send a small-town girl into a twitter.

Charlotte clapped with all the rest of the population of Adams County as the lights and loud music came up, the cameras on their long booms started moving about like elongated teeter-totters, and a pleasant-looking man who reminded Charlotte of a politician and presumably was not Cindi Slate came bounding out on stage and into the lights.

"*Goooood* evening, Bedford Falls!"

He drew out the "good" like a game show host, and the crowd greeted him enthusiastically, though strangers to this part of Nebraska often made the same mistake about their town's name by adding "Falls" to just plain "Bedford." Hannah's theory was that most people knew the classic film *It's a Wonderful Life* was set in the fictional town of Bedford Falls.

Tonight, though, it didn't seem to matter. The emcee introduced them to the Cindi Slate cookbooks and how-to DVDs on sale, as well as the discounted subscriptions to *Cooking with Cindi* magazine, complete with all the recipes and hints Cindi would be sharing that evening. He reminded them that only a small percentage of tapings ever made it to the actual show, but that Visa and MasterCard were always welcome. Charlotte noticed Melody taking frantic notes on the back of an old church bulletin she had pulled from her pink purse.

But they hadn't come here to see the quick-talking emcee, and it wasn't long before the music came up once again behind his introduction of Miss Slate—a pretty, thirty-something thing with blonde bangs that seemed to constantly find their way into her eyes.

Charlotte wondered how Cindi Slate would manage to cook with hair in her eyes, but the audience greeted her like she was a rock star. Over the next ninety minutes Charlotte had to admit, Cindi Slate was quite entertaining, and she did manage to present several clever ideas about cooking ahead and combining ready-made ingredients. The stuffing with wild rice, hazelnuts, and cranberries looked vaguely interesting, perhaps even worth a try someday. Her ideas for using turkey leftovers seemed a little impractical, though. Worse yet, her holiday pies relied on store-bought crusts and fillings. Hannah looked over at Charlotte with a wink and a knowing expression that seemed to say, *Not around here.*

Twenty minutes later, Charlotte tried to wait patiently while Melody and Hannah stood in line to have their cookbooks autographed.

"How about this!" Melody bounded back to the water fountains where Charlotte had agreed to meet them. She waved her cookbook in the air before reading it aloud. "'To Bedford's finest restaurateur. Keep cookin', Cindi.' I got a subscription to her magazine too."

"That's very nice." Charlotte slipped her purse strap up

higher on her shoulder and turned toward the exits. "An early Christmas gift?"

"To me." Melody beamed. "I think you'll be seeing some of these recipes on the menu pretty soon."

By this time the crowds had started to thin. After all, it was nearly nine, and Bob would be wondering what was taking them so long. Thankfully, Hannah also checked her watch as she joined them.

"Except for the pies," Hannah announced, tucking her own purchase under her arm. "It would be embarrassing to serve Cindi Slate's pies to anyone who's ever tasted Charlotte's. No one makes apple-caramel pie like you, dear. Or cherry-berry or pumpkin-streusel. Not even Cindi Slate."

"Well." Charlotte held up her hand to fend off the praise. "I'm sure her pies were more for on-the-go. People like recipes they can make in a hurry, and they can't always put the time into them. You know."

They knew. But Hannah wasn't through.

"In fact, Charlotte." Hannah led the way out of the building, only this time she walked backward so she could face them as they stepped out into the cold. "While all that cooking was going on in there, I had a wonderful idea about your menu at the restaurant, Melody."

"About my menu?" Melody smiled. "I'm afraid to hear it."

"No, you're not." Hannah held up a warning finger as they approached their cars. "Because this is going to make you famous."

"Like Cindi Slate?" asked Melody, still smiling. She stuffed her book purchase in her purse.

"No, no. But I'm serious. What's the one thing people can't get enough of during the holidays—and the one thing you don't serve?"

"I don't serve a lot of—" Melody started to answer, but Hannah cut in.

"That's right. Pies. I mean, you've had them before, but not *Charlotte's* pies. And since Charlotte makes the best pies in the state of Nebraska, why not have her bake you a few, maybe just for Thanksgiving? You can sell them, kind of like on consignment."

Hannah looked at Melody, and Melody looked at Charlotte.

"Why not?" Hannah continued. By that time they'd reached Charlotte's little Ford. By the dim streetlights, the replacement windshield looked good as new—a recent storm had sent a tree branch crashing through the glass. "I'm sure Melody could sell all the pies you care to make, and you two can share the profits. I'll just take a modest commission for bringing it all together."

They all laughed at her joke, but perhaps the idea of a small pie concession wasn't all that far-fetched. Still, Charlotte raised her eyebrows tentatively just to show she wasn't trying to lobby on her own behalf.

"I wouldn't want to presume," she told them. "And it would take a lot of time."

Now Melody jumped in. "Then what if your grandkids helped you? You could even call it the Heather Creek Pie Company. Your grandkids could earn a few extra dollars for Christmas. Don't you think they would like something like that?"

If she only knew.

"Sounds as if we have it all figured out, Melody." Hannah looked to Charlotte. "But what about you, dear? Would you really consider it? Please tell us you would. I mean, the last thing we would want to do is pressure you, but honestly, the world needs your pies, and they need them at Mel's Place. I mean, not that the menu isn't wonderful as is, but . . . you know what I mean."

Charlotte's mind raced as she thought of all the work it would take. She knew better than most cooks how much time she devoted to the baking of just one or two pies for her own family. And these weren't with store-bought crust or canned fillings, either.

Yes, it would be an undertaking. Even so, Melody's idea to involve the kids might work—especially with a financial incentive. She was fairly certain she could talk Christopher into helping, though the other two might be more of a challenge.

"Bob and I have always wanted to involve them in our work a little more," she mused, hardly loud enough for the others to hear. "It might be good for them if they could work together on a common project. And I could work with them, instead of them just working alone."

"There you go." Hannah spurred her on. "A family project."

"The Bedford Pie Lady." Melody was still trying to brainstorm names. "That's too casual. Bedford Pies, Inc. No, too corporate. Maybe . . ."

"I still like 'Heather Creek Pie Company,'" said Hannah.

"I'll let you two come up with a name," Charlotte put in,

stamping her feet at the cold, "if you really think it's that important. But if this is an official invitation, I think I could bake you a few pies to start. A sample of three, just to see if people will really like them."

"Like them?" cried Melody. "I can tell you right now, Charlotte—"

"But if you want more than that, I'm going to have to ask the kids, to see if they'll help. I wouldn't just volunteer them for this kind of thing, and it would just be until Thanksgiving, no later. Oh, and I assume Bob will have an opinion. It *is* a big commitment."

Melody still nodded in excitement, undeterred.

"You do what you have to do, dear, but I think it's a wonderful idea. Like Hannah said, it would only be up until Thanksgiving, at least to start. We can see how it goes from there."

Just until Thanksgiving. Charlotte thought she could handle that. Couldn't she? Melody patted her on the shoulder as she went on.

"And don't think I haven't thought to ask you before, dear. It's actually crossed my mind more than once. I just always assumed you were too busy taking care of your family, and the farm, and Bob's health. I was afraid to ask."

Charlotte couldn't answer, though it seemed quite thoughtful of Melody to put it that way. Normally, yes, she would have been too busy.

"I think," Melody began, then corrected herself. "No, I *know* my customers will love whatever you bake. There's absolutely no doubt in my mind."

"I don't need a permit of some kind?" Charlotte wondered aloud, and Melody waved a hand at her.

"Don't you worry about that. I have all the permits I need."

"Well, perhaps I could try."

"Now you're talking!" Melody literally jumped up and down as if their team had just won the state championship. "See? I knew you were going to thank me for inviting you tonight, Charlotte Stevenson! It was predestined."

If it had been anyone else, Charlotte might have looked askance at a grown woman acting like her granddaughter. But in this case, Melody was just being Melody, and they couldn't help but laugh as the restaurant owner said goodnight and hurried off to her car, twittering and singing as she went. After they climbed into Charlotte's dusty white Ford Focus, Hannah ticked off a list on her fingers as the vehicle sprang to life.

"Apple-caramel first. Everyone *adores* that one. Naturally, plenty of your wonderful pumpkin-streusel pie for Thanksgiving, which will be here before we know it, and then your cherry-berry, which is to die for. You absolutely must give Melody plenty of the cherry-berry. I can tell you right now, that's what's going to put the Heather Creek Pie Company on the map. But, oh dear. Are you able to get the blueberries from somewhere this time of year? Never mind. You're making me hungry all over again. This is going to be fabulous, Charlotte. Absolutely fabulous."

Fabulous probably wouldn't be the first word that came to Charlotte's mind. Instead, her panicked thinking went to her pantry as she mentally scanned the shelves for ingredients.

Shortening, flour, sugar, fresh Granny Smith apples . . . She obviously didn't have enough on hand and would have to restock right away. Bob might have something to say about her turning the kitchen into a pie bakery. And she had no idea where she would find all the berries she would need.

What's more, Melody hadn't even mentioned anything about how much she would pay. Charlotte could call her again in the morning. What had they called it? The Heather Creek Pie Company. Catchy.

The biggest thing, though, would be recruiting her helpers and training them. If she couldn't do that, she would have to stop at three pies and leave it at that.

What's more, if they were going to have any pies ready anytime soon, it would all have to happen . . . yesterday.

"Did you hear me, Charlotte?" Hannah raised her voice above the low hum of the road and the crackle of gravel under their tires as they turned onto Heather Creek Road.

"Oh!" Charlotte realized she had been driving but not paying attention. "I'm sorry. I was just in my own little world there for a moment. Did you say something?"

Hannah laughed. "I said, if you need any help with the business end of this venture, you just let me know. I was thinking you might want to print up some flyers or something. Melody would want to place a special ad in the *Leader*. And I'm sure you're going to thank us for this."

A pair of headlights approached as they continued into

the dark countryside, punctuated only here and there by the lonely lights of a farmhouse.

"I'm sure I will too," Charlotte replied. "I just wonder what I'm getting myself into."

Chapter Four

Christopher squinted as he added an antenna to the attack UFO in his drawing. Another couple of squiggles would make it look even cooler and give it even more warp drives. There. He guarded his masterpiece behind the opened *Mathematics Level Five* text at the front of his desk and slouched a little deeper before he looked around carefully to see what everybody else in Miss Rivkin's fifth-grade class was doing. No sense calling more attention to himself than necessary.

The girl sitting in the next desk, Rachel Wells, fiddled with her math paper, chewed the end of her pencil, and frowned at him, but he pretended he didn't notice. He couldn't help it if she didn't know how to do long division. Really, it wasn't that hard.

In the seat ahead of him, Justin Taylor groaned softly, like he was in pain. Justin looked as big as a sixth grader and he probably had to shave every morning, so Christopher figured maybe he'd been held back a year or five. But did the quiz really hurt that bad?

Most everyone else in the room still had their noses buried in the three pages of math problems, which Christopher had finished five minutes earlier. Over on the right, at the far side of the classroom, a boy named Dylan stared off into space. Every few seconds he would flinch and blink, like someone had snapped him on the nose with a rubber band. Christopher had never seen anyone act like that. He had a funny last name, too, something to do with trees. And Christopher thought he looked Mexican, like a lot of the kids back in San Diego had been, only not quite.

He wondered. But probably it wasn't okay to ask where Dylan's family was from or what was wrong with him. Probably it was the kind of thing he would get suspended for, like bringing a squirt gun to school just for fun. That had happened back in San Diego once, and back then his friend Marshall had known a boy who had known the kid who was kicked out of school for the rest of the year.

Come to think of it though, Christopher thought maybe being suspended might not be such a bad thing. Maybe Sam and Emily could get themselves suspended too. Maybe they could all be suspended together, and then they could all get on a plane and fly back to San Diego, and their mom would be waiting for them instead of being buried in a shiny black box. He would have to think about that.

"Christopher?" His teacher, Miss Rivkin, looked over her glasses at him, brushed a wisp of red hair from her forehead, and motioned for him to come forward. "I need to speak with you for a moment please."

Justin snickered from behind his own math paper.

"Busted by the Boss," whispered Justin, only loud enough for Christopher to hear. Christopher ignored the jab and hurriedly folded his drawing before lowering his textbook shield. He stuffed the drawing into his pants pocket before peering up and pointing at himself with his most innocent *Who, me?* expression.

"Yes, you." She smiled, and he wondered what kind of trouble he was in this time. Justin (and everybody else in the class) didn't call Miss Rivkin "The Boss" for nothing. "And please bring your artwork along."

Oh. He paused for a moment, wondering if it was too late to play dumb about the drawing. No. Their teacher probably had hidden surveillance cameras mounted in the light fixtures, the way he'd once seen in a movie. He sighed, stood up, and stepped over Justin's outstretched foot. On the other hand, he did his best *not* to avoid the end of the pencil hanging over the edge of Justin's desk, but just swept it off as he hurried by.

"Hey!" By the time Justin protested, Christopher had already reached the front of the room, and he kept his face straight. Sam called it his poker face, but Christopher didn't know what it had to do with poking anybody. Not that he didn't want to poke Justin every once in a while.

Right in the eye.

"All right, everybody." Miss Rivkin motioned with her hands down to everyone else in the room. "Let's just finish up the quiz. Quietly, please."

That left Christopher fidgeting in front of her large desk in the corner of the room. She had surrounded herself with loaded bookshelves and posters of cats, musicians, and Einsteins with funny moustaches. She put her large green gradebook aside and held out her hand.

"May I see it, please?"

He knew what she meant, and she knew he knew. He swallowed hard, dug out the UFO drawing, and handed it over.

She would send him to the principal's office for messing around when he should have been doing the extra-credit work she'd assigned him. But she didn't know how boring it was to figure columns and columns of long division when he could be designing the ultimate hyperspace craft. He waited as Miss Rivkin unfolded the paper and studied the drawing.

"This is very good, you know." She finally smiled and handed the drawing back to him. "Next time we have an art lesson, perhaps you can work on it some more then. In the meantime, I'd like you to do something else."

"Okay." He assumed she meant the worksheet of ugly division, the one she gave anyone who finished the quiz early. But she shook her head.

"Actually, I had something special in mind." She rose to her feet and told the class she'd be right back as she motioned for Christopher to follow her out to the empty hallway. When the door closed behind them she crossed her arms and studied him.

"This is pretty easy for you, isn't it?"

Trick question. If he answered yes, then she would find a way to make it a lot tougher, and that would not be good.

If he answered no, well, that wouldn't quite be telling the truth. Either way, as Justin Taylor had told him, he was busted. So he shrugged his shoulders.

"*Hmm.*" With one eye she glanced back through the window in the door, probably to make sure Justin and his gang hadn't set fire to their desks.

With the other eye she kept track of Christopher squirming uncomfortably, and it sort of reminded him of one of those lizards that could see in two directions at once. Not that Miss Rivkin looked like a lizard really. She finally broke the silence.

"When I was your age, my family moved around a lot too. My dad used to be in the air force."

"Sam says we're going to find my dad."

He could have bit his tongue as soon as the words were out of his mouth. Shoot. She'd made him say that, but Sam had told him not to say anything about finding their father —not to nobody, ever. He clamped his fists together, determined that he would not be tricked into saying anything else. But she just nodded and acted as if she understood. Maybe she wouldn't tell.

"Sam sounds like a nice big brother. And I hear your sister takes good care of you too. That's good that you three stick together. But listen . . ."

She stooped carefully, licked her finger to touch up a spot on her shiny brown shoes, and went on.

"What I was going to say was, I know it's hard to make friends when you move to a new place. Especially a place like this, where it seems like everybody already knows everybody, and they were all buddies since they were in preschool together, and they don't really need any more new friends. Do you understand what I'm saying?"

Christopher thought for a moment about how much he should say to her. Not only did this lady have swiveling eyes, and eyes in the back of her head, and surveillance cameras everywhere, but she was also a mind reader. At least, she seemed like she was able to read his.

"I guess so," he finally admitted. Maybe it wouldn't hurt to say that much.

"I know you do." She nodded. "So here's my idea, and you tell me what you think about it."

He waited for her to explain, afraid that she might tell him more about himself, like a palm reader at a carnival who would tell him the future he really didn't want to hear about. He kept his hands clasped tightly behind his back, just in case.

"I know you try not to stick out, but you're ahead of the rest of the class by a few months, at least in math. I think your teachers in San Diego must have pushed ahead a little."

He didn't know anything about that. All he knew was that long division wasn't as hard as Justin Taylor and Rachel Wells and the others thought it was. He waited, not quite knowing what to expect.

"So I don't want you to do the boring extra-credit sheets anymore."

What? That got his attention. He looked up at her with shock and thought she was smiling just a little. Her eyes were anyway.

"Really?" he asked.

"Really." She nodded. "But that doesn't mean I don't have something for you. Instead, I'd like you to tutor Dylan Lonetree in his math."

"Oh." He knew there was a catch. But she held up a finger.

"Now, hear me out, Christopher. I think the two of you might have a few things in common, and I know you could help him catch up to the rest of the class."

Dylan Lonetree with the weird . . . whatever it was? Christopher swallowed hard. Not that he cared about what people like Justin and Rachel would say—although he'd heard them both say mean things to Dylan in the lunch line and out at recess.

Hey, Dilly Brain.

They would say the same thing to him if he agreed to this. And the way Dylan flinched and jerked, and the little snorting sounds he made sort of freaked Christopher out.

"I can't—you know, catch it or anything like that, can I?"

She smiled and shook her head.

"No. That's a fine question to ask, but I guarantee you Dylan's condition isn't the kind of thing anyone can catch. Not in a hundred years."

He breathed a little easier.

"In fact," she told him, "Dylan's a really smart kid, just like you. I think you two will get along just great if you give him a chance. It's just difficult for him to sit still long enough to learn or to read. You've noticed that, haven't you?"

He nodded as she went on.

"I try to help as much as I can, but you know a teacher can only do so much. He needs someone like you."

She paused, maybe waiting for his reaction, but he wasn't sure what to say.

"Well," she finally told him, "speaking of sitting still, we'd probably better get back inside, before Room 7 explodes."

By this time Christopher could hear shuffling and giggling, even through the door. Miss Rivkin pulled it open, pointed toward the center of the room, and raised her "Let's straighten up!" voice.

"Mister Taylor!" she barked. "I leave you alone for three minutes, and look what happens. Would you like me to collect your paper right now and mark it with an F?"

Justin obviously did not and whimpered something about needing to sharpen his pencil as he slithered back to his seat. Only five more minutes until lunch anyway. The wall clock above the door had nearly slowed to a stop, the way it did twice every day—right before lunch and just before the end of school.

"You don't have to tell me today, Christopher," she told him as he slipped back behind his own desk. "Think about it and tell me by tomorrow though, all right?"

He nodded as a couple of kids looked at him with questions on their faces, but by now the period was wrapping up and one by one the rest of the class stepped up to deliver their completed quizzes. Even Justin. After returning from a showy delivery of his quiz paper, waving it about and getting everyone's attention, he leaned his head backward over Christopher's desk, as if he was stretching.

"You in trouble?" he whispered over his shoulder, like he had a right to know.

Christopher glanced over at Dylan Lonetree, who jerked and grimaced again before crumpling a piece of paper and breaking his pencil in half.

"I think so." Christopher finally sighed. "Yeah. I'm in trouble. Big trouble."

Chapter Five

Charlotte hummed "Amazing Grace" to herself as she carefully rolled out the crust to her second pie, the apple-caramel. Already the wonderfully pungent aroma of baking pumpkin filled the house, letting her know that pie number one was coming along nicely, and the ingredients to pies number two and three were arranged neatly before her on the counter. Better not to let Bob know how much she'd spent that morning at Herko's Grocery, however, at least not until she started bringing in profit. She hoped that would be soon.

In the meantime she smiled as she worked, sprinkling a little more flour onto the counter to keep the pin rolling freely, remembering her mother-in-law Mildred's advice.

Use ice water in the crust. That had been one of Grandma's secrets, and hers, as well. Bob's mother had happily lived out her days in the apartment where Pete now lived, singing hymns in her warbly falsetto and baking pies in the compact custom kitchen her son had fashioned for her, complete with a modern double oven that probably didn't look quite so modern these days.

In her final years, arthritis had prevented Ma Mildred from using her hands much, but in a way that had opened an unexpected door of a relationship between the old woman and Charlotte. Before she died, she had passed along to her daughter-in-law what she knew about baking the best pies in the county.

Roll and flatten, not too thin, not too thick. Don't work it too much or you'll make it tough. Charlotte could almost hear Ma Mildred's frail voice explaining the finer points of her art. And today as Charlotte formed the pretty fluted edges around the rim of the glass pan, she couldn't help smiling. She was, as Bob would say about his favorite Huskers quarterback, *in the zone.*

A quick check through the oven-door window told her the special recipe pumpkin-streusel pie was nearly done. At this heat, she might give it three more minutes. A tiny crack had formed in the top, and the crust had goldened nearly to the point of perfection. But like Ma Mildred, she never used a timer. Better to "feel" a pie than to engineer it.

"Just like Ma," Charlotte said softly.

The phone rang, and she nearly lost hold of the to-be-baked pie. She had been expecting a callback from the county extension agent, and she quickly slid the pie back onto the counter and grabbed the receiver off the hook.

"Hello?"

Of course that would be the minute the kids stormed home from school. Sam tossed his backpack onto the counter in between her baking, setting the example for Christopher, who immediately started asking where

Lightning was. She tried to keep Sam from curiously opening the oven, but he missed her wild gestures.

"Mrs. Stevenson?" said the voice on the phone. "This is—"

"I'm terribly sorry," Charlotte replied. "Could you hold for just a moment, please?"

"Smells great, Grandma," Sam told her. "What is it?"

"No, Sam!" Still holding the telephone in one hand, she waved him off with the other and pushed the oven door closed. "Not yet!"

Christopher and Emily gathered around the oven to see what all the fuss was about while Pete burst through the back door as well. Sometimes Charlotte was certain her younger son could smell food cooking from halfway across the county if the wind was right. He tilted his head back and took an audible breath.

"Mom's world-famous pumpkin-streusel pie!" he announced, slamming the door behind him. "You kids haven't lived until—"

"Please, Pete." Charlotte held her hand over the phone and held it out for him to see. "I'm on the phone."

"Why didn't you say so?"

But he did fall quiet as he joined the rest of the pie audience, and Charlotte finally took her call.

"So sorry," she apologized once more. "Are you still there? The moment the phone rang everyone decided to descend on the kitchen."

Charlotte waited for an answer as she cradled the receiver on her shoulder and picked up a couple of hot pads. She would have to pull out the pumpkin pie after all.

"Not to worry, Mrs. Stevenson." The young lady on the other end of the line chuckled. "I have young kids myself. I know what it's like."

As the caller introduced herself, Charlotte decided against explaining that these were her grandkids she was talking about. "I did find out the information you asked for," the caller continued, "although I think you might not like the news."

"Oh?" While cradling the phone in the crook of her neck, Charlotte grabbed the pumpkin pie as delicately as she could with a couple of potholders. She knew she should have used her heavy-duty oven mitts.

"Actually, I called the state department of agriculture, just to be sure I had my facts straight. They confirmed what I thought I knew."

"Okay . . ." Charlotte felt the heat biting through the pad, felt the pan slipping, and tried her best to swivel and find a place for the hot pie on the counter.

"State law prohibits using a home kitchen for baking pies that will be sold commercially. Remember the gal a couple of years ago who started a cookie business at home? Rick Barnes did an article on her a couple of years ago in the *Leader*, but unfortunately someone mailed a copy to someone else at the department of ag. They shut her down faster than you can say—well, you know what I mean."

Charlotte knew.

"Hold on!" Finally the pie slipped through her fingers and dropped between two mixing bowls. Pete reached in to help keep it from melting a hole in the countertop, but his hands looked as if he'd just been digging in the dirt, and she waved him off and slipped a hot pad underneath. He would have burned his hands anyway. He shrugged.

"I'm sorry," Charlotte told her. "I'm not usually this distracted. But could you explain that again? Are you saying that I can't bake pies in my own kitchen?"

"Not if they're to be sold in a restaurant. The only exception is if you have a separate kitchen that's solely dedicated to the baking."

"Another kitchen?" Charlotte stood in the middle of hers, feeling as if the wind had just been let out of her pie-baking sails. "I can't imagine too many people have a separate kitchen just for baking pies."

"Some do." The woman sounded apologetic, but what else could she say? "I'm sorry."

"No, that's quite all right. Not your fault."

Charlotte thanked her and hung up.

"What was that all about?" Pete wondered. He held his hands behind his back this time but leaned in for a better whiff of his favorite pie. "Something wrong?"

"Well . . ." Now Charlotte wondered how much to tell them. She'd hoped to explain the whole thing this afternoon, with the kitchen full of tantalizing aromas. She'd taken care of the aroma part, but now it looked like it was going to end there. She looked around at the kitchen and sighed. So be it.

"That was Vicky at the extension office," she finally explained, and then added a quick rundown on the idea for the Heather Creek Pie Company, Melody's offer, even how they might have earned a little extra Christmas money.

"But now," she concluded, "it's a moot point. Vicky told me we have to have a separate kitchen for the pies, or we can't sell them. So I'll just finish these three and then you kids can eat them yourselves, I suppose."

Pete faced her with arms crossed.

"We'll eat the pies, no problem." He grinned. "But you *do* have a separate kitchen, Mom."

She stared at him, trying to figure out what he meant.

"Grandma's kitchen?" he said. "Don't tell me you didn't even think of it."

He pointed in the direction of his apartment over the barn, where Ma Mildred and Les Stevenson had lived out their last years. True enough, the little kitchen had once been used for pies and a lot more.

"But that's your apartment, Pete. You've been living there for years. I wouldn't think of intruding."

"Well, it's not like I ever use the kitchen. Besides for storage. If that isn't a pie-baking kitchen, I don't know what is."

"Do the ovens even work?" Charlotte wondered if Pete had ever used them for anything other than the occasional frozen pizza since Ma Mildred passed away. He couldn't have been older than sixteen when she died, and more than that number of years had passed since then.

"Yeah, well, the ovens ought to be in a museum, but last time I checked, they fired up good and hot. I think that was a few years ago, but still . . ."

Charlotte thought about it for a moment and then allowed a smile to cross her face the same way she had when Hannah and Melody had talked her into this crazy idea in the first place. Once again, the thought struck her—

Maybe this could work.

"See?" Pete wiped his hands on his pants and gave everyone a smug smile. "We'll make this work. You've got the secret recipes, you've got the pie kitchen the way the ag department wants, and you've got two apple peelers—I mean, cook's assistants—and a delivery driver. What else do you want?"

Sam brightened up a little at the mention of a delivery driver.

"I could drive," Sam said. The sixteen-year-old would probably do anything to actually get his license and get behind the wheel. He was signed up to take his road test next week. "And I got a B on my last history exam, if that matters."

"Well . . ." She still wasn't so sure about intruding on Pete's space, but he wasn't taking no for an answer.

"Come on. You said your friends thought it was a good idea. We think it's a good idea. You can teach the kids what Ma Mildred showed you. You need to just go for it."

"And you'll let us keep part of the money?" Christopher wanted to know. Emily looked interested in the answer as well.

"I wouldn't make you do something like this," Charlotte answered, "unless we all agree. I don't know how much money we're talking about, but don't forget this would be above and beyond your regular chores. So you'd have to get your chores done, too, *before* you worked on this."

"I'm going to put it in the car fund," announced Sam. That was the first Charlotte had heard of such a fund. "And

I guarantee you I am not going to get me a lame pickup truck."

Just then Bob poked his head into the back door. Cold air filtered in, mixing with the warm, pumpkiny aroma.

"In or out!" Charlotte told him, so he pulled his frame inside and balanced on the floor mat in his muddy boots, closing the door behind him.

"I thought you were just coming in for a drink of milk, Pete." He sniffed the air the same way everyone else had done, and a knowing look crossed his face. "Oh, I get it. The pie woman trapped you in her snare. Well, we've still got some work to do on that tractor, you know."

"Grandpa, we've got a business meeting going here," Christopher told his grandfather matter-of-factly. "Sam's going to get his license and earn enough to buy a Porsche 911, and I'm going to get a wireless weather station so I can predict tornadoes before they get here, and rainfall and stuff. I don't know what Emily is going to get. Maybe an iPod."

"Hold on, Christopher," Charlotte laughed. She had hoped they'd take to the idea, but not quite like this. "I don't think you understand what this is all about."

Bob cocked his head sideways at her.

"What *is* it all about?" he asked. "Doesn't sound like the same thing as what we were discussing last night. Thought you were just going to bake a few extra pies for Melody for Thanksgiving."

"Well," she admitted, "I think it just got a little more complicated than that, and—"

"Yeah, Dad," Pete added. "You want to buy some stock in the company?"

"—and I would welcome a little help from the kids." Charlotte finished her sentence.

Bob frowned. Obviously the pie aromatherapy wasn't quite taking hold the way she'd hoped, at least not on her husband. His face looked the same as it did when Pete was setting the irrigation system in a way Bob didn't quite approve of.

"We're setting her up in Grandma Mildred's old pie kitchen," explained Pete. "By order of the Nebraska Department of Agriculture."

"What?" Bob squinted at his son. Pete just pointed back at his mother.

"Ask her. She's the one who's following all the rules. So we're probably going to be setting up worker's comp, too, and retirement plans for all the help, 401Ks. You know, getting their taxes and withholding all set up?"

"We're going to pay taxes?" said Christopher.

"Pete," Charlotte put in, "now you're getting silly."

"You said you're going to pay them, aren't you?"

Christopher's eyes lit up as if he were counting pre-hatched chickens once more. Well, Pete certainly wasn't helping matters much.

"So before you know it," he added with a wave of his hand and a radio announcer's voice, "we're going to be the biggest pie-baking operation in Nebraska. Or Adams County, for sure. Charlotte Stevenson and her grandchildren, Pies-R-Us!"

The three Slater kids followed this exchange like a tennis

match, from Grandpa Bob at the door to Uncle Pete by the oven, talking up the venture as if it were all his idea. Even Charlotte wondered what they were getting themselves into now. Pies-R-Us? Finally Bob halted the volley with a raised hand.

"I don't know what you're trying to get across here, Pete." He pushed the door open behind him, allowing a rush of cold air back inside. "But if it means there's pie for dessert tonight, guess I won't be complaining much."

Pete finally sighed and nodded.

"I'm just trying to get some vision going here, Dad. A little vision never hurt nothing. Fact, I saw this guy on TV the other day, and he was saying as how we've got to visualize success."

"What I'm visualizing right now is you and me getting that tractor fixed. Coming?"

Without waiting for an answer Bob pulled the bill of his cap back a little tighter over his head and stepped back outside. A blast of wind rattled the back-door windowpanes, leaving Charlotte to preside over the pie mess and wonder if she had just received a stamp of approval from her husband. Charlotte looked at her crew.

"So . . ." she managed, straightening up the bowls and swiping at a stray smudge of flour on the counter with a dishrag. "Does this mean I have three volunteers?"

"We're in—aren't we?" Christopher promptly raised his hand while Emily and Sam exchanged wary glances. But Charlotte wanted to hear it from their own lips, so she waited.

"Sam?" she dared to ask.

"I guess we could do it for a few weeks." Sam shrugged as if he could take it or leave it, just like he could take or leave anything else on the farm. Then his eyes brightened again, as if he remembered. "And if I can get my license."

Emily finally nodded her agreement, which was probably the best Charlotte could expect.

"Pete!" Bob poked his head inside once more.

"Coming!" Pete buttoned his coat back up, obviously not hurrying as much as his father would have liked.

"You really think we could make some money?" Emily brought up the subject one more time, and Charlotte didn't blame her.

"Melody thinks we can," answered Charlotte. "But then, Melody's been wrong before. We'll just have to step out and let God take care of what happens."

"Well, I think we ought to start moving equipment over to the new kitchen." Pete picked up a couple of empty mixing bowls and placed one on his head like a helmet, just to be silly. "For the next few weeks we're going to be in pie heaven, folks."

"Right now you'd better go help your father with that tractor," she told him, taking back the bowls. "And keep your dirty hands off my mixing bowls."

"Yes, ma'am." He smiled as he bowed out of the kitchen backward, stumbling a little on the threshold. Christopher giggled.

But pie heaven? In a way, Charlotte hoped he was right. After all, what was the alternative?

Chapter Six

"No, look. You have to do it like this." Christopher sighed and wondered how he had let himself be talked into sitting in the back of the room with Dylan Lonetree, wrestling with long division. "Hasn't the teacher ever showed you?"

Dylan pressed his lips together and turned a lock of long, jet black hair around his finger, like he was winding up the rubber-band propeller of a toy airplane. He shook his head briskly. He wasn't giving Christopher much to go on, was he?

"Never had no—" Dylan paused at an odd time as his face contorted and he gasped for breath. Dylan was obviously used to his own tics, but Christopher gripped the side of his desk and did everything he could not to recoil.

"Nobody else who wanted to explain it." Dylan finally labored through the words, punctuating them with squints and twitches. Sometimes the words came in machine-gun bursts, as if they'd been saved up for hours and could only find their way out with great effort. Other times they seemed to hide just below the surface, trapped behind the boy's contortions, waiting to escape.

Christopher wondered how the kid could ever sit still long enough to work through a single problem, even a totally simple one like three hundred divided by twenty. Dylan's pencil squiggled across the page as he motored through yet another series of tics accompanied by soft grunting noises.

Just to be sure they didn't need to call 911 or something, Christopher glanced over at the front of the room, but Miss Rivkin just smiled and nodded at him, like everything was okay.

Well, it was not okay, and Dylan Lonetree made him nervous, though he wouldn't admit it. The kid couldn't keep his pencil still on a single column of numbers, which might be half his problem.

"Okay, look." Christopher finally had an idea. "We're going to try something different. Turn your paper sideways."

Dylan did as he was told, and Christopher helped him darken the lines on his paper to use as double-wide columns. Maybe if he had a bigger place to put his numbers, thought Christopher, he might not get them so jumbled.

"Cool." Dylan smiled at the new arrangement, though at first he still seemed to lose track of what he was doing between all the twitching and distractions. Even so, gradually he started to catch on, and eventually he did work a rather simple problem all the way through without wandering from column to column the way he'd been doing.

"Way to go." Christopher nodded. "Maybe we just need to set it up the right way."

"Maybe." Dylan nodded and looked sideways at his work. It still snaked around the page a little, but eventually he had ended up with the right numbers. And that, it appeared, was more than he had been able to do on his own.

Christopher wasn't sure what to do next, and Miss Rivkin was helping a group of advanced kids with their assignment.

"So, are you going to keep helping me?" Dylan started on another problem, and Christopher shrugged.

"If I'm here. I don't know. My brother thinks we're not going to stay in Bedford very long."

"Where you going?"

"Can't say for sure. I liked the ocean in San Diego. We went to Sea World once and saw a bunch of cool killer whales. Maybe we'll go back there. My mom used to take us to the beach, before . . ."

His voice trailed off. He hadn't meant to say anything like that, not here at school, and certainly not here with Dylan Lonetree. But Dylan didn't seem to notice, or care.

"My stepdad's always moving us around," he told Christopher. "We lived in Omaha, and Tulsa . . ." He ticked off the locations on one hand. "Two places in Lincoln. Says he's getting a better job, but I think he gets fired a lot. So we have to move. Sometimes we leave in the middle of the night. We just grab stuff and put it in the car, and we're gone."

Christopher wasn't sure how to respond, except that he recognized the feeling, sort of. A couple of months ago Sam had told him that was just how he intended to leave the farm, only he hadn't said anything like that lately.

"When we were in San Diego, we lived in three different apartments from the time I was in kindergarten. I went to two different schools."

"You too?" Dylan looked at him as if someone finally understood him. "That's awesome. Everybody else in Bedford is like, they were born here and their great-grandfather was born here and they're never going to move. Me, I went to four different schools before we came here where my aunt lives."

"No way. I've never met anybody who's moved more than me."

"Yeah, well." Dylan shrugged and grinned. "Now you have."

"But we'll probably move again pretty soon," Christopher told him. By this time he didn't recoil in alarm when Dylan began twitching or making odd noises. "I heard my uncles talking to my grandfather, and one of them was telling him he has to sell his farm. So I don't know if I can keep helping you out."

"Whatever." Dylan shrugged again as he slipped his math book and paper back into his desk. He raised his head to the air and sniffed. "I'm going to be first in line. Hamburgers today."

"Really?" Christopher sniffed, too, but didn't detect anything except the usual classroom smells of books, chalk dust, the aquarium in the corner, and smelly gym shoes on the floor next to him. But Dylan gave him a knowing look, as if he was used to Christopher's reaction.

"My ma says 'cause we're mostly Dakota Sioux and some Winnebago we can smell things better."

"Winnebago?" Christopher gave him a closer look, at the dark eyes, dark hair, and honey-colored skin. Maybe that explained the other boy's different last name too. "Isn't that like a motor home? I just thought you were Mexican or something."

"Shut up. We're not Mexican." Dylan snorted. "And they

stole our tribe's name without asking. There was Winnebago people a long time before there were cars and motor homes and stuff."

"Sorry. I just thought—"

"That's what everybody thinks." Dylan pushed his chair back and got up as Miss Rivkin signaled for the class to line up at the door. Lunchtime couldn't have come too soon.

Christopher hurried to grab his own lunch sack out of his desk and lined up with the others. He still couldn't smell hamburgers, or any other food for that matter. Maybe Dylan was making it up. But as boys gathered in one line and girls in the other, he noticed the big pink lunch announcement flyer tacked up by the light switch. Monday, it said in big block letters, was hamburger day with french fries.

Aha. So this time Christopher breathed deep and looked over at Dylan.

"You smell those fries?" asked Christopher.

EMILY STOPPED AS THE OTHER KIDS in her class hurried out of the cafeteria and into the hallway. A disgusting burger swimming in fat and rivers of oozing mustard lay half-eaten on the fold-out table next to the remains of an even more disgusting corn dog that someone had smashed for fun. It reminded her of roadkill.

If I don't do something about this, she told herself, *nobody ever will.*

And besides, there was Mr. Duncan, the principal, chatting with a few students and couple of the lunch ladies. Emily didn't see the pastor's wife, Mrs. Evans, which was probably a good thing. Mrs. Evans didn't work in the lunch line every day, only once in a while. Maybe she was a sub. But no way would Emily have the courage to do this if Mrs. Evans was standing there too.

Maybe this was her chance.

"You coming?" Her friend Ashley paused just outside and looked back.

Emily waved her off. "You go ahead. I'll just be a few minutes."

Ashley paused for a moment, and then nodded and let the double doors slam behind her. Emily took a deep breath and walked back over to where Mr. Duncan stood. What was the worst thing that could happen?

It wasn't long before the principal noticed her. "How are you doing, Emily?" Mr. Duncan looked down his rather long, straight nose and smiled at her. Everything about Mr. Duncan seemed long and straight, from his long neck to his long, wiry fingers. "Are you liking your teachers?"

How was she supposed to answer *that* question?

"Sure." Emily tried to think of the most polite thing to say. "Mr. Baird is really, uh, funny."

In a dorky sort of way, but she didn't think to add that part. Her ninth-grade science teacher thought jokes about the totally disgusting little fetal pigs in disgusting jars of disgusting formaldehyde were a scream.

Mr. Duncan just beamed, rocking back and forth on the heels of his tennis shoes. Someone should tell Mr. Duncan that white tennis shoes just didn't go with dark dress slacks and a cashmere sweater.

"He's everybody's favorite," said Mr. Duncan. "I'm glad you like him too."

She kept the smile on her face, and he probably noticed her fidgeting.

"Is there anything I can do for you, Emily?"

"Well, actually." Emily felt herself talking faster and faster as she blurted out the words. "I had an idea I wanted to tell you about."

Mr. Duncan's eyebrows arched, and he leaned a little closer.

"I always like to hear ideas from students. What's on your mind?"

Emily paused when she noticed the kids standing close by were listening too. Well, so what?

"I was just thinking about the food we get at lunch here. You know, in the lunch line."

Mr. Duncan nodded toward the two lunch ladies, who had returned to cleaning up the kitchen and were preparing for the next group.

"Oh? They do such a good job, don't you think?"

"Yeah, I guess. I mean, that's not what I mean. I was just thinking, instead of always just serving high-fat stuff like corn dogs and hamburgers and fries, maybe we could offer some vegetarian and organic stuff as well. That way, people could have a, you know, choice."

"Oh! You mean like veggie plates. We do have veggie plates."

"I know. But nobody ever eats way-microwaved cauliflower and dead broccoli. I'm talking about like, main dishes with, you know, stuff that's better for you. I have a recipe for a low-fat tofu-spinach lasagna. You know, that kind of thing."

One of the kids who was listening in giggled, but then her friend tugged her arm and they hurried for the door. Emily sighed. Maybe Principal Duncan didn't get it either. But he did guide her to the door.

"I think that's a wonderful idea, Emily."

Emily looked up at the principal.

"You do?"

"Yes, I do. And I have to say, it's not the first time I've heard the suggestion, though it is the first time I've heard it from a fourteen-year-old."

"Well, back in San Diego, we used to have some of the same gross—I mean, some of the same kinds of things as we do here. But a few of the parents complained, and the school board made them change it."

"Hmm." Mr. Duncan nodded as they walked down the halls. "I have to tell you, making a change like this isn't easy. Mainly it's a budget issue, and the district only gives us so much for our lunch program. We can hardly make it work as it is."

"But it doesn't have to be more expensive, does it?"

Again Mr. Duncan smiled as he pulled her aside to step into the main office.

"Here's what I can promise you: I will definitely bring it up at the next school board meeting, and see what kind of options we might have. If anything develops, you'll be the first to know, all right?"

Well, that sounded fair, sort of. Emily nodded and returned the smile. How hard had that been?

She didn't actually find out until a couple of minutes later, as she was returning to her locker, and a couple of the biggest ninth-grade girls blocked her way.

"Uh . . ." Emily pointed to her locker directly behind them. "Excuse me?"

Neither of them made any move to step aside. She recognized the larger of the two from church, Nicole something, even though the girl had totally ignored her until now. Emily would never say it out loud, but either one of the girls could have played on the boys' football team.

"Do you have a problem with our food?" Nicole crossed her arms over her chest while the other girl looked on. "I hear you're trying to get rid of corn dogs and burritos. What if some people like it the way it is?"

Emily could hardly believe it. These two girls couldn't actually be defending the school cafeteria menu, could they? And who said anything about burritos?

"Uh . . ." She wasn't sure if she could play dumb or not. "Not change it. Just try to get some more choices. That's not bad, is it? More choices?"

"If you don't like our food," said the other girl, stepping forward, "you should have just stayed in California, where you could eat all the raw fish and toe-foot you want."

"You mean sushi and tofu." By this time Emily was heating up. Somebody hadn't taught them how to be polite. And they didn't even know how to pronounce "tofu."

"Whatever." Nicole kept her arms crossed, and by this time, a small crowd had gathered around them. "My mom says new people like you need to be a little less picky about what you eat and just appreciate what you get."

Emily thought this was a pretty bizarre argument, and who was this girl's mother anyway? Maybe she should have known, but she didn't. At this point she didn't care.

"Well," she snapped back, "I could appreciate it a whole lot more if everything wasn't swimming in a pool of grease when it hit the plate. You're not honestly telling me you *like* that stuff, are you?"

She probably could have modified that last statement about "swimming in grease," but by now she had crossed her arms, too, and the crowd was beginning to murmur, like they were expecting a fight.

"You don't even eat the cafeteria food, newbie. What do you care?"

Emily's heart began to pound. Surely not here, in the middle of the hallway? But she'd never been in a real fight before, so she couldn't exactly know what to expect. Kids back in San Diego had fights in school all the time. Mostly boys. But if she got into one here, Grandma would kill her. And with a girl from church, no less.

"So you want to get rid of our Coke machine too?" someone piped up from the crowd, and everybody laughed.

The good news was that the noise attracted the attention of Mr. Baird. Out of the corner of her eye, Emily could see the tall, gray-haired science teacher hurrying toward them.

But before he could arrive to break up the confrontation, someone else had grabbed her by the arm and swung around in front of her like a shield. Ashley!

"Why don't you girls leave her alone?" said Ashley, pulling Emily back into the crowd even as she spoke. "She's not hurting you."

By that time, Mr. Baird had arrived on the scene, and immediately everyone tried to look as if nothing had happened.

"What's going on here?" he asked. By that time most of the kids were disappearing back into the passing hallway crowds as quickly as they had appeared.

"Just getting ready for class, Mr. Baird." Nicole played the innocent part rather well. "Are we going to dissect the fetal pig again today?"

Mr. Baird rubbed his chin and surveyed the thinning crowd with a suspicious look, but he had obviously arrived too late to make any arrests. As Ashley guided Emily down the hallway, Emily couldn't help looking back one more time. Nicole and her friend were laughing with Mr. Baird as if nothing had happened.

"What is wrong with you?" asked Ashley. The ringing lunch bell meant they had four minutes to get to class, and they hurried. "I leave you for five minutes, and you almost start World War Three with Nicole and Sarah."

"I didn't do anything to them."

"No? Well, you sure made them mad about something."

"That's the crazy part. They acted like I was doing something evil just because I asked Mr. Duncan if we could have a better lunch menu. You know, like with some vegetarian options. You'd think they would thank me instead of beat me up."

"Oh." Ashley hit her head with the palm of her hand and nodded. "You know who Nicole's mom is?"

Emily shook her head no, so Ashley went on.

"Mrs. Evans. You know the pastor's wife whose feelings

you hurt when you trash-talked her? Mrs. Evans who works in the school cafeteria a couple days a week?"

"Oh." Emily's heart sunk. "*That* Mrs. Evans. I never made the connection."

"So Nicole just thinks she's sticking up for her mom and the Great American Way, see?"

"Yeah. Only, how come everybody in this town is related to everybody else? I thought there were laws against that kind of thing."

Ashley laughed and shook her head.

"You're crazy, you know that? And if you think they get mad at you for attacking cafeteria food, wait until they think you're attacking their third cousins."

"I'm not attacking anybody. But . . . oh no." Emily groaned and dug in her heels when they reached the door of Mr. Baird's science room. He had already passed them and disappeared inside. "My book. I forgot my book."

This normally might not have been such a big deal, but in Mr. Baird's class, arriving on time with the textbook in hand and the latest assignment was one-fourth of their grade.

Emily considered stepping into class without her book and without the assignment in hand.

What does it matter? she asked herself. *We probably won't be here by the end of the semester anyway.*

But she just couldn't do it. Instead, she turned back the way they'd come, back through the thinning crowds.

"You're going to be late, Emily," Ashley called after her.

Emily waved back at her only friend as she hurried down the hall. Yes, she would be. And as she ran, she wondered how much a plane ticket back to San Diego would cost.

Chapter Seven

Charlotte closed her eyes as she shut off the ignition in her little Ford, praying quietly for strength to get through this without breaking down. How many years had it been since she was in this same parking lot, in this same situation, worrying the same worries?

She couldn't count the number of school plays she and Bob had attended here, or the times she had volunteered to bring cupcakes for special events. Or back-to-school nights and open houses, when they'd come to sit in tiny chairs next to low tables and concerned teachers explained how Denise could be doing so much better if she'd only put in more effort. Or that Pete was really very bright if he would only pay more attention.

Funny that most of the memories involved Pete or Denise, hardly ever Bill. Pete was the one who got into a scrap or sprained his ankle on the playground equipment, clowning around. Denise, she recalled, got the attention of her teachers for writing on her arms to impress the boys or for failing the occasional test when an emotional blowup with friends took precedence over anything else in life.

The girl was never quite living up to her potential, as her teachers would always say.

Bill, on the other hand, quietly made all A's and Bs and earned more than his share of Student of the Month awards. Frankly, she understood how living in the shadow of such a big brother could have been a challenge. She had had an overachieving big brother herself. Still, it never diminished her own pride in her elder son's accomplishments, not in the least. Any parent would be proud of the son who made good. She just understood how tough it could have been for Denise. She thought about how it might have been different, if only . . .

She caught herself staring at one of the trophies in the glass case, from the year Bill had participated in some kind of math Olympics. At the time, everyone had oohed and ahhed at all the college offers and scholarships he had earned while Denise remained in the shadows, more troubled than anyone could have guessed.

A mother should have known. She accused herself all over again. *I should have done something while there was still time. Sent her to a Bible college, perhaps. Kept her away from the wrong crowd. Listened to her more.* Hindsight.

Charlotte glanced once again at the glass case full of trophies on her way past the office, remembering the spelling bees and the math-a-thons, and the basketball tournaments. She stepped carefully around the imposing memories to the room where Christopher's teacher had said she'd be waiting after school.

A couple of younger children—second graders, perhaps—chased each other through the hall, shouting and laughing. She paused at the door to Room 7, remembering again the times Denise's teachers had called her in, in this very same way.

Had anything really changed? Never mind the wrinkles on her face and the age spots on her hands, chapped from a morning of scrubbing and cleaning her "new" bakery kitchen. She rapped lightly on the door, peeked through the little wire-reinforced window, and saw Miss Rivkin wave at her to enter.

"Mrs. Stevenson!" The earnest young teacher smiled at her from her place behind a standard-issue gray desk. Perhaps it was the same one Denise's teachers had once used. "I really appreciate your stopping by."

"Not at all." Charlotte glanced at her watch. "Although I probably shouldn't be staying long. I left word with my son Pete when you called, but if it's at all possible I do like to be there when the kids get home."

"I wish more parents were like you." Miss Rivkin smiled pleasantly and pushed aside a pile of papers she'd obviously been grading. She wore her hair short, possibly dyed red, and tied casually behind her neck, with a navy blue skirt and a cream-colored blouse. Probably not the kind of style that Charlotte would ever wear, but very professional. "Too many of them are just, well, they don't have time for their kids."

"Well, you know." Charlotte wasn't sure how to answer or if she should agree. "People are very busy these days."

"That's why I admire you, Mrs. Stevenson. I mean, I know you care. Otherwise, you wouldn't have taken in your three grandkids. I don't know if I told you before, but I want you to know as Chris's teacher how much I really admire that."

"Thank you." Charlotte nodded awkwardly, still waiting for the punch line. Erin Rivkin hadn't called her here to present a Grandparent of the Year award. Charlotte cleared her throat nervously.

"So . . . is Christopher doing all right?" she finally asked. "I try to ask him every time he comes home from school, but he really won't share with me much. Just bits and pieces, and I have to be listening carefully or it's too late. You know what I mean?

"Oh, yes." Erin, *Miss Rivkin,* pulled out a drawing and handed it to her, as if she was making a corporate presentation. "In fact, that's part of the reason I asked you to come by this afternoon."

Charlotte nodded knowingly as the teacher went on. Perhaps it was the way she dressed or spoke, but something intimidated her about the young Miss Rivkin.

"You see in some areas he's far ahead of our other students academically. He's very interested in space, in planets and UFOs, and such. Very clever at math and science, for the most part, and I see him testing out in much higher percentiles. But the surprising part to me is that he's quite an artist, don't you think?"

Charlotte admired the detail of the drawing, the ears and noses, even down to the fine hair. Yes, she had to admit it was very good.

"But that's not the problem, right?" Charlotte had to hear for herself.

"Correct." Erin nodded and for the first time seemed to fidget just a bit in her chair. Apparently this was getting closer to the real point. "He seems in many ways—on the surface—perfectly happy. But in so many other ways, I just know he's still grieving, trying to cope with the loss in his life. But he's still not there yet, and I'm not sure if there's anything else we can do about it. On the whole I'd say he's quite withdrawn and doesn't seem able to make friends very well. I'm sorry. I don't mean to be blunt."

"No, that's quite all right." Charlotte nodded. "You know he's very attached to his older brother and sister. I'd hoped that he would make more friends by now though."

"Perhaps you could encourage him more that way?"

Charlotte nodded, aware of the failure staring her in the face once again. Hadn't Denise's teachers told them the same thing once? It had been so long ago.

"So he doesn't have any friends, is that it?"

"Actually—" Erin's face lit up a little. "I do have some positive news to tell you in that regard. I've just asked him to help tutor another rather shy boy who doesn't have any friends either. Your Christopher is helping him with his math skills."

"Really?" Charlotte raised her eyebrows in surprise.

"Actually, that's why I wanted you to stop by. I watched them out of the corner of my eye as they were working in the back corner, there. The other boy has some, ah, physical challenges. I probably shouldn't say this, but the kids know he's on more meds than I can keep track of, to tell you the truth. Family's just moved into town, and from what I can gather, they've moved around a lot. Actually, I shouldn't have said that. Let's just say it's kind of a tough family situation, but your son—I mean, your grandson—"

Charlotte smiled at the slip of the tongue. Well, there was a compliment, if she ever heard one.

"But they're getting along?" she asked.

"I think they are, so far. Maybe they have some things in common since neither of them grew up around here, like so many of the other kids did. I mean, it would be good for Christopher to make other friends, but this is a start."

"You mentioned . . ." Charlotte hesitated, wondering if it was any of her business, or if the school had privacy laws they had to follow. Well, it wouldn't hurt to ask. "You mentioned this boy has physical issues?"

"Ah yes." When Erin looked directly at Charlotte, the young woman's dark eyes sparkled pleasantly. "I suppose it's no secret, exactly, and you'd certainly know what I mean if you ever met him."

"I understand." Charlotte wasn't sure she did.

"All I can say is that I believe he has a condition related to Tourette's syndrome. So it's, um, a lot of twitching, and he has trouble keeping his attention on his speaking or on a book, for example. It's profoundly affected his learning abilities, and he's . . . well, let's just say he's probably not where he should be academically."

"I don't mean to be nosy." Charlotte almost wished she hadn't asked, but not quite. Now she understood.

"Not at all. But as I was saying, I could see Christopher was hesitant to get close to Dylan at first, just like a lot of other kids in the class. Dylan's appearance can be disconcerting."

"Dylan. I see. But they seem to be okay together?"

"Christopher is patient. I'm already seeing that. I have a feeling he's going to turn out to be quite a good little tutor."

"When she was young his mother always said she wanted to be a teacher . . ."

Charlotte's voice dropped off, leading to an awkward silence. Better not to wade into emotional deep water here.

Fortunately Erin seemed to sense her discomfort as she rose with Charlotte to walk her to the door.

"Don't get me wrong, Mrs. Stevenson: Christopher still has plenty of roadblocks to overcome, particularly in his social skills. He doesn't always pay attention. Sometimes it's like he's on another planet. But that's not why I asked you to come. I'm just hoping you could encourage him since this arrangement may turn out to be as good for him as it is for Dylan."

Charlotte nodded. Well, that was good news, wasn't it? Certainly not as ominous as she'd feared.

"Well, I appreciate knowing about this." Charlotte shook Erin's hand and said good-bye and then stepped back out into the hallway with a sigh.

Well, she told herself, *I survived that one.*

She straightened her hair and marched back down the hallway, weaving her way through a troop of giggling girls in blue sweatpants and mismatched basketball jerseys, all running down the hallway, on their way to the gym for practice. Sixth or seventh graders, probably.

"Excuse me!" said the lead girl, and they nearly bowled Charlotte over in their enthusiasm. She held up her hands and turned sideways to avoid the river of green. And even in all the confusion, she couldn't help hearing her name called out.

"Mrs. Stevenson!"

As the crowd thinned, Charlotte turned to see Dana Simons navigating her way, loaded down with an armload of papers. For a moment Charlotte thought the young teacher would drop them all right there in the hallway. And then it occurred to her—

"Why, Dana. I thought you taught across the street. You're still Sam's . . ."

"Third period English teacher, that's right." Pete's former girlfriend fell into step beside Charlotte as they both headed down the hall toward the exit. "They were going to shuffle a couple of periods around, but turns out I'm still his teacher. But our main copy machine over there at the high school jammed this morning, so they said I should use the one here in this building until it's fixed."

"I see." She noted the top papers, stapled together. *"A Midsummer Night's Dream*?"

"It's our Shakespeare for the semester. Did Sam tell you? We're going to do a readers' theater."

Charlotte shook her head. "No, he didn't say anything. But it's funny. I did the same play when I was that age."

"Really?" Now Dana was interested. "Did you play a part? Do you remember any of the lines?"

"I don't remember a thing." She closed her eyes and tried to recall, but after that many years, the memory was lost. "All I remember is I played a fairy. Um, what was the name?"

"Peaseblossom?" guessed Dana as Charlotte shook her head no. "Cobway? Moth?"

"No, none of those. It was something with a seed. Mustardseed! That's right. Just a tiny part."

"Ah, but you know what they say, how there's no such thing as small parts, only—"

"Only small actors."

Dana smiled. Charlotte had always liked the young woman.

"By the way," Dana shifted the conversation and the

papers in her arms as they left the building and headed into the parking lot, "I heard you're starting into the pie business."

"Oh?" Charlotte sighed in relief at the change of subject. "Word gets around, does it?"

"You know how it is. Melody's talking it up with everyone. You can tell she's excited."

"Well! She isn't wasting any time, is she? And I haven't even delivered the first pie yet."

"Doesn't seem to matter. All the teachers are lining up for preorders. You have quite a reputation, you know."

"Preorders! Melody didn't say anything about preorders." Charlotte tried as best she could to brush aside the compliment. "But you're always welcome to come by the house for a sample, you know. I mean, we're in the middle of gearing up for this Thanksgiving rush, but you could, well—"

What was she saying? Charlotte bit her tongue, not wanting to sound like she had just invited Pete's old flame to dinner. But there was no mistaking the blush in the young woman's cheeks.

"Actually, um, I assumed perhaps Pete had already mentioned it to you?"

Charlotte tried not to look as flummoxed as she felt. Whatever was this girl talking about?

"Oh, dear." By this time poor Dana appeared positively mortified and held a hand to her cheek in alarm. "He told me it would be perfectly all right. I'm terribly sorry. I shouldn't have agreed."

"I'm the one who's sorry, dear." Charlotte smiled in a vain attempt to lighten the mood. "I have no idea what you're talking about."

"Um . . ." Dana cocked her head to the side, much like a puppy trying to make out a strange sound. "I'm coming over to help Pete with the paperwork to apply for his GED classes. And then . . . he said I should stay for a bite to eat? Friday evening?"

Well. Pete had obviously been making inroads that he had told no one about, least of all his parents. And now if he had already invited Dana to dinner, well, all the better. Saved her the trouble. It would have been nice if he had let his mother in on the secret though.

"Dinner. Of course!" But by then the comedy of the encounter overtook Charlotte, and she couldn't help giggling. "You mean, at our house? This Friday? I mean, tomorrow evening? That's a wonderful suggestion, even if it's the first I hear of it! And I'm so glad about, you know, the classes and all."

Dana caught the giggle as well.

"So he didn't tell you." She shielded her mouth but couldn't help it either.

"I'm afraid not."

"I am totally embarrassed," Dana gasped, and now she sounded more like a girl Emily's age than a proper teacher with everything under control. She nearly lost all her papers in the process.

"Well," Charlotte replied between laughs and drying her eyes. "I am so pleased that you'll be coming. But I'll tell you: I'm going to have a talk with that young man."

She left still giggling, getting a strange look from the high school principal, Chad Duncan, who was just getting into his SUV parked out on the street. Well, but that was all right. Charlotte hadn't expected to avoid anyone by coming into town this way.

"Oh, Charlotte?"

Charlotte paused at her little car as the principal called over to her.

"Several of our staff ordered your pies this morning," he told Charlotte. "I was the first one to sign up for the cherry-berry. Does that mean I'll get the first one out of your oven?"

"I don't know about the first, but you'll be sure to get the best."

Even though she was smiling, Charlotte felt a chill run up her spine before she could coax the heater in her car to life. Melody really hadn't said anything about pre-orders. And Principal Duncan's pie was another that Charlotte hadn't even begun to bake.

Chapter Eight

"You like?"

Sam jumped at the sound of the older boy's voice, and the boy laughed that he had startled him.

"Uh, yeah." Sam backed away from the jet black sports car parked horizontally across two parking spaces in the far corner of the student parking lot Thursday afternoon. "What's not to like?"

"That's what I'm saying." The older boy grinned and hit his remote, causing the car to chirp as it unlocked. "It's for sale, you know."

"Yeah, a couple of people I know told me." Sam relaxed a little, daring to run his hand across the chrome of a rear-view mirror. He was not about to admit that he knew absolutely nothing about cars—only that he wanted one, badly, and this one looked very cool. The main thing was that it was not a pickup truck and it would get him to school or to town in style. "I was kind of looking at buying a car, and thought, maybe, you know . . ."

"Cool." The other boy slipped into the driver's seat and started up the engine with a roar. "So you want to take a test ride? Maybe you need a ride someplace?"

Was he kidding?

"Uh, no, actually I'm going to be getting my license tomorrow, but I was waiting for the . . ."

He was about to say *bus*, but thought better of it. No way could he tell a senior that his grandparents made him take the bus to and from school. In fact, he was probably the only kid left in his grade who did. Or it seemed like it at least. He stared at his reflection in the car's shiny paint job.

"On second thought, sure." Sam hurried around to the passenger side. He might not get another chance like this. Why not? This way, he'd probably get home way earlier than Emily and Christopher anyway. Emily might wonder, and he probably should have told her, but oh well.

"So, which way you going?" The tall boy had managed to slip his long legs under the steering wheel. Sam thought he was on the varsity basketball team, but he couldn't be sure. Half the boys in the school either played football, baseball, or basketball. Sometimes all three. "Uh, Heather Creek Farm? I'm Sam. We just moved here from . . ." He hesitated again, wondering how much to say. But the driver didn't look like a lot of the other farm kids. He wore longer hair that reached down to the collar of his varsity green and gold jacket. The name Jason embroidered on the front probably served as all the introduction he ever needed. And he wasn't carting around hay bales in the back either.

"From San Diego."

"No kidding? San Diego's a cool place. Always wanted to go there. So do you surf?"

"Some of my friends did."

Jason left a patch of rubber behind them as he screeched out of the parking lot. Sam noticed Jason hadn't fastened his seat belt, so after hesitating a moment he left his unbuckled too. He had to hang on to the door as they rocketed down Goldenrod Street, around the other side of the high school. Jason turned up a fancy CD player, loud, letting out a chest-thumping rhythm.

"I had that put in last year," he yelled over at Sam. "Three hundred and fifty bucks."

"Nice!" Sam's throat went dry at the figure, already close to what he had scraped together so far for his own wheels. Most of it was from back in San Diego—birthday money, odd jobs, that kind of thing. Maybe he didn't want to ask how much Jason wanted for his car after all.

"So this is the GSX, which is the cool model with the turbo. It'll blow the doors off a Mustang." Now Jason was starting to sound a little like a car salesman as he shouted over the thump of the CD player. "Two-point-oh-liter turbocharged, five-speed, and . . ."

He added a few more incomprehensible numbers that sounded impressive to Sam. He would have to read up a little more on this kind of car.

"So why are you selling it?"

"What?" Jason inclined his ear, inadvertently turning the steering wheel with him as he leaned.

"I said, uh—"

Sam felt his eyes widen as he pointed at the road ahead of them, which Jason didn't seem to care much about. They nearly sideswiped a couple of mailboxes before Jason brought it back under control.

"Never mind." Sam shook his head and thought again about buckling his seat belt or asking how many accidents Jason had been involved in. But now Jason was showing him how the turbo worked, passing a tractor and a slower-moving small white Ford that looked extremely familiar.

"I've had it up to a hundred and twenty," said Jason, "and it'll go better than that. You want a fast car, this is it. In fact . . ."

As Jason went on about the virtues of his vehicle, Sam sunk down as low in his seat as he could, bringing his right hand up to shield his face—just in case the driver of the Ford looked his way. But it was probably too late.

"Hey, you okay?" Jason looked over at him as they jetted down Route 12 and eventually turned onto Heather Creek Road. Sam was afraid to look over at the speedometer.

"Never better." He finally straightened up as they approached the farm, and he pointed out their driveway. "Up there. Take a right."

"Here?" Jason would have skidded past the road had he not jammed on the brakes, sending gravel flying. Fortunately he eased down the lane as if he suddenly realized grownups might be watching.

"So what do you think?" While Jason pulled up in front of the house, Sam could only think of the little white Ford that would be pulling up behind them in a moment or two.

"Uh, fantastic." Sam jumped out as fast as he could. "And I really appreciate the ride."

"Here." Jason wasn't done yet. "Let me pop the hood and show you the engine. It's—"

"Er, actually." He glanced at the driveway. Nothing yet.

"Maybe I can look at it after school. Tomorrow. Yeah, would that work? I, I really have to run. You know, chores."

"Sure. Whatever." Jason revved it up and eased back into gear as he turned the car to leave. "See you around."

"Thanks again." Sam waved and then turned to sprint toward the barn.

Unfortunately, he hadn't gone more than a couple of steps when Jason's car ground to a halt and backed up to overtake him. Jason sounded the horn, and the passenger side window rolled down with a hum. What now?

"Forgot your book." Jason extended a science text out the window, which Sam grabbed with a nod.

"Right. Thanks."

By this time Grandma's Ford had turned down the gravel lane and was headed their direction with a kind of tortoise-and-hare determination. Sam didn't stay to make any introductions, though, only skipped backward and nearly bumped straight into an empty rain barrel before he found his way into the barn and abandoned his science text in a corner. It would be better, he thought, if he went incognito for the next couple of hours.

As bad luck would have it though, that's when Uncle Pete walked out from the back of the barn, staggering to keep his balance behind an oak dining table.

"Hey, perfect timing." Pete stopped and started to lower the load. "Grab the other end of this table, would you? I just about killed myself picking it up. We need to walk it over to my place."

"Uh." Sam looked over his shoulder and out the half-open double doors to where Grandma Charlotte was parking her car over by the back door of the main house.

"Come on!" Pete grunted his impatience and nodded at the table. There was nothing to do but lift the other side and walk with Uncle Pete out the barn and over toward the shed with its second-story apartment where they were setting up the pie-baking. He held his breath the closer they walked, and he could tell his grandmother wasn't moving from her spot where she had parked herself next to the car, waiting.

This could not be good.

CHARLOTTE PRESSED HER LIPS TOGETHER, mapping out a list of cool, calm, and reasonable questions to ask Sam. Surely he would have a good explanation. Perhaps he had been kidnapped and was taken in the sports car against his will.

Sam walked by with Pete, carrying a table through the yard.

"Sam."

The two furniture movers stopped. Sam looked intently at the tabletop.

"Explain to me what just happened back there," she said.

She set down her box of home-canned cherries on the table right where they all stood, between the big house and Pete's apartment.

Pete obviously had no idea what was going on, though he kindly set down his end of the table when Charlotte blocked his way.

"What's going on?" he asked. "Somebody in trouble? I haven't seen your face so red since I dented Dad's car, and that was back when I was his age."

"I had nothing to do with it, Grandma." Sam raised his hands in surrender. "I swear."

"Just tell me what you were doing riding in a car that was going at least eighty miles an hour down a country road." She labored over each syllable. "I thought it was going to blow me right off the highway."

"You saw me?" His voice squeaked now, and he cowered as he backed a couple of steps.

"Let me count the ways." She started a tally on her trembling fingers. "First I saw you riding in this car, and I'll tell you, it was the shock of my life. Then I saw you try to hide your face. And by the way, it didn't appear that you were wearing your seat belt. What were you thinking?"

"Wow." Pete whistled long and low. "That's pretty impressive, seeing all that in a car that's doing eighty."

She ignored her son's commentary and kept her glare focused on Sam. She'd seen what she'd seen. Sam fidgeted, staring at his shoes and kicking at a tuft of stray grass.

"I'm really sorry, Grandma," he finally said. "But see, I was just checking out his car in the parking lot in front of school, and he came out of nowhere and told me he would give me a ride home. Like, I wasn't even asking or nothing, just looking."

"Out of nowhere." She echoed his excuse but waited for him to say more.

"And I didn't know he was going to pass all those cars. He was just showing me how the turbo worked in his Eclipse."

"An Eclipse, huh? Is that what that was?" Pete sounded impressed. "What year?"

Charlotte cut off the car talk with a cool glance, redirecting her question to Sam.

"Did you ask him to slow down?"

He shrugged vaguely. She supposed he could have lied and said yes. Perhaps they were making progress.

"What was his name?" she asked.

When he told her, Pete hopped back into the conversation.

"I know who that is. His dad owns a half-dozen gas stations between here and Grand Island." Pete leaned up against the table. "The Gentry family, now they've got money. Daddy probably got him a new car . . ."

"Pete." Charlotte kept her gaze on Sam. Finally she caught her breath and felt the anger gradually slipping away. Maybe it was from watching her grandson squirm in discomfort, from seeing his genuine embarrassment. Perhaps it wasn't entirely his fault. No, she didn't suppose it was.

"I want you to promise me something, Sam."

Every year they heard of another senseless tragedy on the local roads, usually a young driver showing off and losing control. Sometimes alcohol played a role, heaven forbid, but usually it was simply a combination of too much speed and too little experience. Last year a car full of teens from Harding landed upside-down in Heather Creek.

She would do anything to keep it from being one of her own. Finally he looked up and met her gaze, and he looked surprised at the tears in her eyes.

"Grandma," he whispered.

She wiped away the emotion and squared her shoulders. Now was not the time to cry, no matter how she felt.

"Promise me you won't accept any more rides from

Jason Gentry. Promise me you'll use your head more than that. Sam, I don't want you getting killed."

"Okay, Grandma. But what if I buy his car?" Sam had obviously regained a measure of courage by this time.

Pete laughed, then made a funny squealing sound with his hand when he covered his mouth.

"Sorry, Sam," he said. "But did he tell you how much he wanted for his wheels?"

"Well, I didn't ask him, but—"

"And if you have to ask, then you can't afford it. Isn't that what they say? Sorry, kid. But in this case I think you're dreaming."

"Well, I'm not going to get a pickup." Sam squared his jaw. "I'll tell you that much."

"Uh-huh. Well then you're going to be saving a lonnng time for the turbocharged, one-point-six-liter—"

"It's a two-liter. It's bigger. It's the GS model."

"Well excu-use me," Pete drawled as he picked up his side of the table once again, this time with a broad smile. "But while we discuss the finer details of Japanese muscle cars, maybe we should get this table in place. It's going to get rained on. Is that okay, Mom?"

Charlotte hadn't noticed, but by this time the gathering gloom had started on the yard, sprinkling tiny ice pellets on their heads as well as on the furniture they'd been moving. But before the boys could move their table away she planted her palms on the tabletop and looked straight at Sam.

"You didn't answer me." She waited while he looked away briefly, then focused back on her. Finally he took a deep breath and nodded.

"I promise, Grandma."

Did he mean it? She waited for only a moment before allowing herself a small smile. But by that time the heavens had let loose with a punishing mixture of cold rain and wet ice pellets.

"So did we get that straightened out?" Pete tugged at the front of the table. "We need to get your table inside, and I'm freezing my tail off, besides."

"Come on." Charlotte grabbed the corner opposite Sam and followed along as Pete led the way to the outside steps to his second-floor apartment. "We have some pies to make, don't we?"

"And I'm the official taste tester!" Pete whooped as they hurried across the yard in the hailstorm, lugging the heavy table and the cherries between them.

Chapter Nine

The next afternoon Charlotte paused to look around once more at her "new" kitchen: long and a bit narrow, its single window looked out over the fallow fields facing the highway. The once-pretty white lace curtains had yellowed a bit, just like the black-and-white-checkered linoleum on the floor and the photos of flowers and sunrises on the wall, but the whitewashed cabinets seemed as clean as when Ma Mildred had commanded this space.

"Hey, Mom!" When Pete stomped up the stairs she could hear that his boots were obviously still on, and she bit her tongue before mentioning the fact. This was, after all, still his place, even if she had commandeered the kitchen for now.

"Up here!" Charlotte called back. She looked around the kitchen for a suitable place to cool another pumpkin pie, her fourth of the day for the restaurant. She shoehorned it in between three others and a box of Pete's junk on the nearby counter.

"So where do you want these?" asked Pete. She couldn't see his face until he peered around the side of a large wooden crate. He actually had one cradled in each arm.

"Ta-da." Pete seemed pleased at what he had apparently built as he set two crates carefully down on the floor next to the double oven. "You're going to like them."

She nodded and looked a little closer. Carrying handles attached to the top and each side, and a protective front cover slid up through a groove to reveal a series of six shelves—large, wide cubbyholes, really. Each of the shelves had side-by-side holes cut out of the middle, about the size of a stove burner.

"It looks very clever," she finally told him. Pete stood next to his creation and smiled. "But—"

"You still don't know what it is?" Finally he grabbed her latest pie from the counter, nearly dropping it with a yelp.

"That one's still hot," she said as she handed him a hot pad.

"Thanks for telling me." He quickly slid it into place on the top shelf, then shook his right hand.

"You didn't give me a chance, young man."

But now she could tell exactly what Pete had built. And as a matter of fact, it was quite nice after all. She could see how this was going to come in very handy.

"So it slides up like this." She worked the front cover up and down while he hoisted it by the top handles.

"Up to a half-dozen pies in one carrier, and it fits right into the backseat of your car."

"You measured?"

"Well . . ." He paused. "If it doesn't we can always shave a little off the door opening of your car."

"Good thinking." She checked her watch before turning back to her second oven and then peeked inside before extracting two more pies. She figured about sixty to seventy minutes per oven, two pies each time. "I'll leave that up to you. But I have to say, this is quite clever. Any girlfriend, if you had one, would be impressed."

He groaned and rolled his eyes.

"There you go again, Mom. Remember my junior prom, the time you and Dad embarrassed the socks off me when you—"

"Pete!" She pulled another carton of eggs from the little Westinghouse dumpling refrigerator. "You're not still going to hold that against us after all these years."

"After all these years, I'm just saying you sound the same today as you did fifteen years ago."

"I'll take that as a compliment."

"Just promise me when Dana comes over tonight that you won't make any comments about how old I am now compared to back then, or how handy I might or might not be around the house, or old girlfriends."

"What does that leave us to talk about?"

"See? That's what I mean. She's just an old friend who's coming over to help me with some of the paperwork for my GED application, okay? And then it just seemed like it made sense for her to stay for dinner, that's all. So don't pepper her with a lot of questions, like 'Where have you been all these years?' or that kind of thing. Okay?"

"You forget I've just recently spoken with her, which is how I knew what you were talking about in the first place. She seemed quite eager to stop by. Everything will be fine."

"Yeah, but it's been a long time, you know."

She softened and paused over her mixing bowl. True, a

lot had happened in the years since a very young Pete had dated his high school sweetheart. A lot of life had passed them by since they'd parted ways.

"You could do a lot worse," she told him. "She's a very nice girl. Woman. Sorry."

"Mom! Enough! How many times do I have to tell you, it's not a date!" He playfully pretended to grab her shoulders and shake. "I let you work in my kitchen, and this is how you treat me."

"Well, I'd hardly call it your kitchen anymore. We'll call it Grandma Mildred's kitchen, and praise the Lord for that double oven. Have you ever taken a close look at it? It was so clean inside—it didn't look as if you had ever cooked anything here in the past few years."

"Microwave popcorn. That's my specialty. I have a running tab at Mel's, and the diner too. Do these hands look like they do a lot of gourmet cooking? I burn water if I try to boil it."

He held out his rough-creased hands, dirt under his fingernails, honest and weather-chapped like his father's. These were the hands of a farmer, and she didn't mind the strength they represented. Liked it, even. The question was, did Dana Simons?

"You know I'm only teasing. But you'd better clean those fingernails, no matter what."

She patted one of the new pie-carrier boxes and smiled at him. "Seriously, these will work really well when Sam is delivering the pies in town. Really. Thank you. And I didn't even ask. What's gotten into you?"

"It was nothing. Just a little scrap lumber."

The carefully trimmed corners, sanded smooth surfaces, and perfect seams told her it was much more than that.

"Well, I do appreciate it, in any case. Oh, and you should have seen what was inside these cupboards. I think they still had Grandma Mildred's things in them from, well, years ago. The only one I couldn't get to was way up there."

Charlotte pointed up to a small bank of cupboards over the sink, just out of her reach, while Pete grabbed a kitchen chair and balanced on it.

"I don't think I've ever seen what's up here either," he said. "She was a little lady, wasn't she?"

"She must have had someone else go up there for her," replied Charlotte, "just like you're doing . . ."

She saw the falling objects before he did, but fortunately Pete had enough sense to duck and cover, when all she could do was screech and scurry away from the clanging avalanche of tin plates.

"Whoa!" Pete teetered in place but held on until the cupboard had disgorged a full load of vintage pie tins, now piled around his chair. He winced when one last tin plate slipped out and banged him on the forehead. "Sorry about that."

But Charlotte happily returned and kneeled to gather her treasure.

"I was wondering what had happened to all those wonderful pie plates." She held one up.

"Oh, is that what they are?" He looked a little closer. "I thought they'd be good for storing nuts and bolts in the shop."

"Not on your life! This will be more than enough for us

to use. And they look almost as clean as the day they were put away. Ma Mildred was good about keeping things clean."

"Oh, so I'm almost killed in this avalanche, and you're looking at how clean the plates are?"

But he slipped off the chair and helped her gather the remaining tins, stacking them on the counter. She made a point of pausing and looking closely at his head.

"I think you'll live."

"Well, then don't forget, you owe me one of your pies for all this help."

"I was wondering when you would ask for payment. You know I do appreciate it, Pete."

When they were done he made a show of bowing, then turned to step back down the stairs. Pete could be a challenge sometimes. But other times, he could charm the bees out of their honey.

"One other thing, Pete?" she called down the stairway. "Could you send the kids over when they get home from school, please? I'm getting to the point pretty soon where I need an extra hand. We need to finish up four more pies before tonight, and I still need to get over to my other kitchen before our guest of honor arrives."

"Extra hands. Check. I'll send 'em over."

"And have Emily bring over another jar of caramel with her when she comes."

"Okay, honey. I mean, caramel."

"Watch it, buster. I know blackmail. And I have plenty of embarrassing stories I can tell your friend tonight about little Petey when he was six years old. Remember on the first day of first grade, when you—"

"I'm leaving now!"

Charlotte smiled to herself as he slammed the door behind him. Unfortunately, she'd forgotten to ask him to check the Crock-Pot back in her real kitchen in the main house. Oh, well. Surely it would be okay, just simmering all afternoon. She just hoped Dana liked beef stew.

Chapter Ten

It's wonderful, Mrs. Stevenson."

Dana smiled as she took another bite of beef stew, breaking the odd silence around their dinner table. She was polite. Just not very honest.

Bob looked as if he'd just been choked. His eyes bulged, and Charlotte gave him her best *don't you dare say a word* expression.

On the other side of the table, Sam and Christopher both seemed to be engrossed in buttering more rolls while Pete rearranged potatoes and carrots on his plate. Charlotte hoped Christopher wasn't feeding Lightning under the table the way he'd tried to do before.

"So, Christopher," Dana broke the silence, "your grandma tells me you're tutoring another student, is that right?"

Christopher nodded and pointed to his full mouth, then mumbled something that sounded like "yeah" and "math."

"I think it's wonderful," said Charlotte before they all fell silent again.

"And, Sam," Dana tried once more, "you're still kicking for the football team, aren't you? You were so good at that."

"*Mmm*, no." Sam chewed on a roll and shook his head. "We were done last month. Didn't make the playoffs this year."

Dana nodded seriously.

"I knew that. I still think you did a wonderful job. I don't see how anyone can kick the ball that far."

"I did get my license though." His face brightened as he dug into his wallet and pulled out a new, laminated prize with NEBRASKA printed across the top in bold blue letters. Dana reached over to hold it and take a look. "The photo is quite handsome."

Charlotte thought Sam turned a little pink as he took the license back and replaced it carefully in his wallet.

"Now all I need are some wheels to go with it," he added.

As the rest of them chattered on about driver's licenses and how well Sam had scored on his exam, Emily carefully picked at her stew.

"There's no meat, dear." Charlotte quietly reminded her. "You don't need to worry."

But no one else seemed to be eating either and Charlotte supposed this meatless stew disaster ranked among the top ten worst.

"This is terrible," she finally admitted.

Bob choked, bless his heart, and Christopher giggled nervously.

"What did you say?" Sam said.

"I said, this is awful, and I apologize for not tasting it before I served it tonight. I should have known when all the water cooked off that it would taste this way. The sauce is terrible, the spices are terrible, even the green beans taste terrible.

"Oh no, Mrs. Stevenson." Dana wasn't giving up the polite approach anytime soon. "It's, it's very good. Maybe just a little . . ."

"A little burnt?" Charlotte finished the sentence for her. "I must really be getting old to not smell something this bad before it went on your plate. Maybe my olfactories are wearing out. Now it's my turn to be embarrassed."

"I didn't know you had old factories, Grandma."

"Dude." Sam poked his little brother in the side as he reached for another roll. "We need to get you one of those little handheld dictionaries, so you know what Grandma is talking about."

"All right, mister smarty." Christopher poked him back just as hard. "Get me one. But what's an old factory?"

"It's this, Einstein." Sam flipped Christopher in the nose to illustrate his point, which set off another round of retaliation. Bob held up his hand for order once again.

Charlotte added yet another apology. "I'm sorry. I was over there in a pie-making fog, not paying attention, until just a few minutes ago. I never noticed the water had boiled off."

She looked at her guest and started removing plates, starting with Dana's.

"This is not the way I usually do things, dear. Pete will tell you that. Things are just a little bit, well, in a tizzy here, lately. Now, how do you like your eggs?"

"What?" Pete's mouth hung open. Well, what was he worried about? It wasn't the first time she'd offered to serve them breakfast for dinner.

"Cool!" Christopher shoved his bowl away. "Scrambled for me!"

"Scrambled for the young man. Now we're talking. "Dana, how about you?"

"Would over easy be all right?"

"She asks if it will be all right!" Charlotte pulled out her largest frying pan. "Pete, tell her it's going to be all right. And while you're at it, tell her about the pie transporter you built for me today. This man is quite the carpenter, you know."

Charlotte smiled inside as she made some toast, began fixing eggs to order, and listened to the animated voices all around the table. Though Sam and his grandfather mostly listened, Christopher and Emily took turns explaining to Dana about all the work they'd done to help make pies for their grandma that afternoon while Dana coaxed Pete into explaining all about the pie carrier and how he'd made it. She seemed appropriately impressed, as Charlotte had hoped she would.

Meanwhile, Charlotte went through a couple dozen eggs—scrambled for Christopher and Emily, sunny side up for Pete, over easy for Dana and Bob.

"Only thing better," said Bob, "would be a couple pancakes alongside, buried in a sea of homemade maple syrup. *Mmm . . .*"

"Don't push your luck, mister." Charlotte slipped three eggs onto his plate. "And you know you can't be eating syrup."

But by this time Emily and Dana were talking like sisters. Dana nodded as she listened to the cafeteria food story.

"You didn't tell me all this," noted Charlotte, wondering what else Emily had kept to herself. Dana seemed to be bringing it all out.

"You should be proud of her," said Dana, "for being brave and speaking out like that. And for all the right reasons too. Kids really do eat too much junk."

Emily beamed at the compliments. Charlotte still wasn't too sure, but she bit her tongue and tried her best to look agreeable. Better not to say anything yet.

"I just thought it would be a good idea to have something in the cafeteria besides the same old stuff," said Emily.

"Not if you get yourself killed in the process," Sam told her, using his toast to scoop up another mouthful of eggs. "I heard you ticked off a bunch of people, and you're saying they should have tofu burgers."

"I never said anything about tofu burgers." Emily dropped her fork. "Although I do have some recipes I'm going to give Principal Duncan. He said he would bring it up at the next school board meeting."

Sam shrugged. "Just remember what happened when you went after the church potluck food."

"Well, sometimes that church potluck food needs a little going after," declared Dana, slipping an arm around Emily's shoulder. "Honestly, there are a lot of people who shouldn't be eating some of those awful casseroles, don't you think?"

When no one answered right away, Dana caught her breath and brought a hand to her lips.

"That sounded rather flippant, and I should not have said that," she whispered. "I'm sorry."

No, she probably should not have, but Emily didn't seem to mind. Judging by the enchanted look on her face Charlotte had no doubt she'd found a sister-in-arms. "Well." Charlotte changed the subject, since they'd all wolfed down their eggs by this time, and Christopher was looking for more. "Let's save a little room for dessert, shall we?"

"Ah, dessert," said Pete. "I always say dessert should come first, before the main course."

"You eat dessert first in this house, young man," Charlotte told him with mock seriousness, "and I'll guarantee you there won't *be* a main course."

"Well, okay." He threw his hands up.

"Speaking of being impatient and eating dessert first—" Charlotte finished up her own eggs and turned to their guest. "—Did Pete ever tell you about the year he opened his Christmas present on Thanksgiving?"

Pete rolled his eyes with embarrassment. "Oh, come on, Mom. Not that story. Dana doesn't want—"

"Pete!" Dana leaned back with a bemused look on her face. "You never told me that story."

"Come on, Pete," Charlotte said. "You were just a little boy. It's a cute story."

"Please," said Dana. "I'd very much like to hear."

"Well, actually," Charlotte continued, "I think he was five or six." She didn't mind making Pete squirm just a little, just this once.

"Four," Pete interrupted. "I was only four. If you're going to embarrass me you need at least to get your facts straight."

Charlotte held up her hand.

"Are you going to tell her, or am I?" She turned back to

Dana. "In any case, he was old enough to know better. It was the year his father had picked up a little model tractor for him at a farm convention, and the cute little thing was sitting in our closet for three months. We were saving it for Christmas."

Pete made a swirling motion with his hand for her to get on with the story. "As I was saying," she went on, "we were saving it for Christmas, so I wrapped it early and hid it behind my Sunday dresses in the closet. But somehow, little 'Dessert First' Pete got wind of the gift. I still don't know how, unless he was spying on his parents."

Pete held up his hands in surrender.

"And do you know what?" she said. "He actually snuck into our closet while I was out in the barn and opened the present right there!"

Dana laughed. "Quite bold."

"The funniest part was how he suddenly had an attack of conscience, so then he panicked and tried to wrap the box back up. He just put it right back where he found it and actually believed we wouldn't notice."

That brought a good laugh from everyone, especially Dana. And Charlotte thought the young woman had a very pleasant laugh, easy and warm. Pete could do much worse.

"Pete's our impatient one, all right." Bob joined in the fun. "But he's not getting his Christmas present early *this* year."

"Oh?" Pete pretended to act surprised. "You mean I actually *am* getting something?"

"Didn't say that," his dad retorted. "Maybe you will, and maybe you won't."

"Don't forget my weather station." Christopher added, and he looked so sincere it pained Charlotte. Would he be too disappointed when he didn't receive one?

"Don't mean to change the subject," put in Sam, which was the first thing he'd said since digging into his toast and eggs, "but when do we get to have some pie?"

"Who said anything about pie?" Charlotte winked at Dana as she cleared a couple of plates from the table. "I have a feeling no one is going to be asking for pie in a week or two, when we're good and sick of it."

"Sick of it?" Pete shook his head. "Impossible!"

"Don't be too sure," she replied. "And don't forget tomorrow is Saturday, kids, so don't be making any plans. I need all hands on deck. Last time I spoke with Melody, she was expecting another party order, so we probably have at least a dozen more pies to bake."

Chapter Eleven

"There's the car I'm going to buy."

Sam grabbed his little brother's arm and pointed with his chin, stopping in the middle of the sidewalk between the equally disgusting aromas of Filly's Flower Shop and the Shear Genius Beauty Shop.

Christopher held his nose and nodded as Jason Gentry's black Mitsubishi Eclipse rumbled by. But Jason didn't notice the two brothers standing on the icy sidewalk.

"Cool." Christopher approved. "How many pies are we going to have to sell before you have enough money to buy it?"

Sam frowned. Christopher would have to ask that.

"A lot, actually. I don't even want to think about it."

"I thought you said you already had money."

"Yeah, nowhere near enough though."

"Not enough to buy the farm either, right?"

"What?" Sam shook his head. "That was totally random. What are you talking about?"

Christopher opened his mouth like he was going to explain, then shook his head.

"Nothing." Christopher could act pretty off the wall sometimes. "Forget about it."

They started toward the bulletin board outside the *Bedford Leader*, where people from town posted announcements for things like church special events, piano recitals, and hay for sale by the bale. They tried to find a place for a flyer about how the Heather Creek Pie Company was taking orders for pies through Thanksgiving. But a middle-aged man with barely any hair stuck his head out the front door of the newspaper office.

"You kids get that poster approved?"

He didn't sound gruff exactly, but Sam wasn't quite sure how to answer.

"Didn't know we had to," Sam finally answered as the man stepped outside and motioned to see what it was.

"Hmm." The man had wrinkled his nose and tipped his head back so he could see through the bottom half of his glasses the way Grandpa sometimes did, but then he nodded like he knew what he was looking at.

"We're good?" asked Sam.

"Melody's running the same ad in this week's paper," the man finally replied. "In a two-column, four-inch, so I don't know how we're going to shoehorn all that information. But we're good. Here—"

He pulled a pen out of his pocket and initialed the corner of the flyer along with the day's date.

"November 8 already." He shook his head. "Thanksgiving's going to be here before you know it."

"We're going to sell enough pies to get a weather station and a GSX," Christopher told the man, who crossed his arms.

"In that order, huh?" He finally cracked a smile. "Well, I don't know what a GSX is, but if you get a weather station, maybe you could supply me with a local forecast. The feed we get is always a few degrees off."

Christopher thought that was a great idea, but since it was too cold to be standing out on the sidewalk, gabbing, the man soon retreated back inside.

"You don't need to tell our wish list to everybody we meet," Sam told him once the door to the *Leader* had slipped shut. Christopher looked up at him with surprise on his face.

"Why not? We're going to get those things, aren't we?"

"Sure. We just don't need to advertise it, that's all."

"But we *are* advertising." Christopher held up a couple of flyers with a grin.

"Right." Sam held his hand out for a couple of thumbtacks, which they placed on their sign, high and in the middle of the board.

"Onward." Sam pointed across the intersection of Bayard and Lincoln at the craft store where his grandmother bought sewing and embroidery stuff. "Grandpa's sister'll let us put something in the window. Then down at the Tractor Supply."

Christopher followed dutifully as they crossed over to Fabrics and Fun, where, with Rosemary's permission, they started to tape a flyer in the lower corner of a front window, next to an old poster from the fair.

"I never have figured out what people do with this stuff," whispered Christopher.

"Shh." Sam didn't blame him for wondering. With all the patterns and fabrics and lacy things hanging on the walls and lining the shelves, this shop seemed like another world. At least it didn't smell funny.

"You tell your grandmother to stop by more often," said Rosemary, the gray-haired woman behind the counter. "We haven't seen her in weeks."

"Sure will," Sam answered, looking for another piece of tape.

She had the same eyes and square jaw as Grandpa, and she held a pair of blue scissors to cut some kind of fabric pattern thingy. Another woman had stopped in to chat, too, so Sam just finished what he was doing and nodded politely before escaping past the cheery door chime.

"EMILY, BEFORE THE BOYS GET HOME, do you think you could print out twenty-five more flyers?" Charlotte dusted the flour from her hands and pointed to where she wanted Emily to stack the washed pie tins. Between Ma Mildred's supply and the new ones she'd bought, she hoped they would have enough. "I just remembered Melody wanted them to go with each piece of pie she sells at the restaurant, or with every whole pie."

"Flyers." Emily nodded and tossed her drying towel to the side. "Check. I have to print out a few recipes too."

"For your crusade?"

"Grandma!"

"I'm sorry. I shouldn't have used that term. I'm actually very proud of you, standing up for what you think is right."

Emily didn't answer, so Charlotte returned to mixing ingredients for the next pumpkin-streusel pie, taking up where Emily had left off. To the pumpkin puree she added sugar, brown sugar, and heavy cream and then stirred in Ma Mildred's special blend of cinnamon, nutmeg, cloves, and ginger. She knew the amounts by memory but announced what she was doing so Emily could perhaps help more the next time.

"Two teaspoons ground cinnamon," Emily echoed. "Is the teaspoon the big one, or the little one?"

Charlotte's eyes widened. Emily lifted a hand.

"Kidding, Grandma. I know the difference."

Charlotte wasn't totally convinced she hadn't meant it, but it was nice to see the lighter side of her granddaughter. Charlotte continued explaining the fresh spices they'd carted over from her home kitchen: a quarter-teaspoon of ground cloves and a half-teaspoon ground nutmeg, then a teaspoon of ground ginger. As Emily took over the mixing again, Charlotte carefully scalloped the edges of another crust and laid it aside, ready for filling.

"The secret is fresh spices, dear, and paying extra attention to the crust. Everyone notices the crust."

"Mm-hmm."

"You have to be sure not to overwork the dough, see? Every time it's reworked, it gets tougher and chewier when it's finally baked. That's what Ma Mildred always told me."

Emily was staring out the window.

"You're following this, Emily?" she asked, just to be sure, and Emily snapped back to attention.

"I'm not Christopher."

The defensive tone of Emily's reply caught her off guard. What had brought that on?

"No, of course you're not. I just—"

"Sometimes you treat me like I'm a little girl, Grandma." Emily picked up one of the measuring spoons and frowned while Charlotte stuttered an apology.

"I'm—I'm sorry, Emily. I had no idea. You know that's not what I mean to do."

Emily seemed to shrug away the apology.

"I know. But another thing, Grandma, I still don't get why we can't use the ready-made piecrusts. Don't they have them at the grocery store? I always thought they tasted pretty good. It would be tons easier."

"And tons faster," Charlotte agreed. "But that's not the recipe that makes this pie special. Otherwise, people might just as well order one from the grocery store."

"All right. But then can't we just use regular nonfat milk, instead of this, like, cream? It's like when Sam left a half-carton of milk out on the counter for two days. Totally gross. I'm sure the pies would taste a lot better, and they'd sure be healthier."

Emily shuddered and made a silly face as she picked up the mixing cup of cream with two fingers, giving Charlotte a chance to laugh.

"Well, there is such a thing as low-fat evaporated milk," Charlotte admitted. "But I've been told by my taste testers that it's not quite the same."

Charlotte smiled. She didn't mind explaining all the basics, if that's what it took. At least Emily was asking, and she supposed that was a good thing. She also didn't suppose Denise had ever had time to teach Emily or the boys about baking.

They would just have to begin at the beginning.

This first batch would just take a bit longer than she expected. With Melody calling every hour to update her pie order, they didn't have a whole lot of time to spare. Eight pies down, four to go, and a pile of apples to peel.

What was taking those boys so long?

SAM AND CHRISTOPHER posted one more Heather Creek Pie Company flyer inside the lobby of the post office and then put up another one at Herko's Grocery Store, on the bulletin board next to a picture of a lost black dog.

"Hey, check it out." Naturally Christopher would notice the lost dog. "Maybe we could find it and get a reward."

"There's no reward." Sam took him by the arm. "Come on. If we see a black dog on the street, we'll pick him up and return him to his owners. They've only been looking for him since—"

He glanced at the homemade sign to check.

"Last February."

"Oh." That let the wind out of Christopher's sails. They made their way to A&A Tractor Supply. Sam had never been inside.

"Isn't that your car?" Christopher pointed at the black Eclipse parked in front. Sam didn't answer, but no, it wasn't his car. Yet. They pushed inside, out of the cold, to see Jason Gentry leaning against the parts counter. He straightened up and pointed at Sam when they walked in.

"Hey, Brad," he told the man behind the counter, "there's your man. I'll bet he needs a job, especially if he's going to buy my car."

"You think so?" The other guy looked interested, though Sam had no idea what they were talking about.

"Uh . . ." Sam waved a copy of the poster at them. "Okay if we put this sign here in the window, next to the other stuff?"

The "other stuff" would be a rodeo poster from last August, a National Rifle Association meeting notice, and a little red sign that read Help Wanted.

"It's for our grandma," explained Christopher.

"Right," said the friendly looking man with slicked-back black hair. "You're the Stevensons' kids, right? Denise's sons?"

Br d was embroidered across the top of his grease-stained blue shirt, next to the A&A Tractor Supply logo of a little black tractor with an "A-A" across the top. The *a* in his name had come unembroidered.

"Yeah," answered Sam. "And, uh, you need help?"

"Brad says he can't find anybody willing to take a job around here." Jason grinned at them. "I told him I'd do it, but with no benefits, no 401K, no way."

He headed for the door.

"That's what they all say. See ya, Jason."

Brad looked like he was used to joking with Jason. "Kids, huh? They're all looking for the cushy jobs with the fat paychecks. Well, maybe somebody'll let me know when they find one."

"What kind of job?" Sam figured it wouldn't hurt to ask. He turned to see Jason give a quick wave as he left the store.

"Afternoon delivery, mostly taking parts out to farms.

Both car parts and tractor parts. I've been having to deliver stuff myself, which means I have to lock down the shop, and I don't like to do that. Either that, or we stop delivery altogether, and my dad started that service thirty years ago. Don't think we're going to stop now. Why, you interested?"

"Maybe." Sam thought for a second. This kind of job would pay real money, as opposed to the loose change Grandma was offering him to run pies to town. It was a business decision, right?

"Well, look." Brad rubbed his hands on a rag as he spoke. "It's not like I'm interviewing, or anything. And you can see there's no lineup of applicants. If you're interested, and Jason here thinks you're okay, I can give you a shot at it for a week or two, just to see how you do. Pays minimum wage, but I'll give you my discount on any part we order through the store for your truck or whatever. You don't have a fancy car like that Mitsubishi out there, do you?"

"Not yet." Sam checked to see Jason driving away.

"I've only got one part here to deliver today, down on Meadowlark, and you could start Monday, officially."

"But—" Sam wasn't sure how to say it. "You don't even know my name."

Brad just laughed.

"I've known your uncle since I was a kid. He comes in here a lot."

I should have guessed, thought Sam. *Everybody in this town knows who I am.*

But the question still hung in the air.

"So you want me to take this part and then come by after school Monday?" asked Sam.

"Works for me." The man grinned and reached out his hand over the counter. "Brad Weber, by the way."

Sam shook Brad's hand, still trying to sort out what he had agreed to do.

"Sam." He nodded. "Sam Slater."

So he had a job. A real job. Sam almost forgot to tape their pie sign inside the window before skipping outside with his little brother. Instead of pie flyers under his arm, now he cradled a box with a tractor alternator.

"What did you just do?" Christopher wanted to know. "Aren't you going to deliver pies for Grandma anymore?"

"Sure I am. But I mean, come on, how many pies are we talking about?"

"I think she wanted us to do other stuff, too, besides just drive the pies into town."

"You don't get it." Sam hefted the box as they passed under a streetlight just blinking on in the late afternoon gloom. "This is a real job, with real pay."

"Grandma said she would pay us."

"Yeah, but when? Two weeks from now? A month? And how much? It all depends on how many pies we bake too."

"She said she really needed the help."

"Yeah, well, you guys are helping. And I said I could do both, didn't I? We just have to run this alternator down to a place at the end of Meadowlark."

"You know where that is?"

"We'll find it. Can't be that hard."

Christopher didn't look like he was convinced, and he frowned as they walked around the block to where Sam had parked Uncle Pete's ancient Chevy truck in an alley where nobody would see it.

"And another thing," he made a note to himself, "I'm not going to name my car something lame, like Lazarus. Cool cars don't have names, period."

"I still don't think it's a good idea, Sam." Christopher shook his head as he climbed up and slid onto the ripped blue vinyl bench seat.

"What are you worried about? I said I can handle it, okay?"

Chapter Twelve

Charlotte put down the phone and glanced over at Emily, standing by Pete's pie transporter. They both stared out the window, waiting for a pair of headlights to come bumping down the driveway.

"Okay, now I'm getting a little worried," admitted Charlotte. "Rosemary just told me they were putting up their posters at Fabrics and Fun over three hours ago. They couldn't have taken that long to get to the rest of the stores in town."

She imagined the inexperienced driver stuck in a ditch somewhere, hurt or worse, and she prayed silently for the boys' safety as Emily paced in front of the window. Emily wasn't about to admit it, but Charlotte guessed she was just as worried.

"Come on, Sam!" Emily scolded the gathering darkness. "That's what cell phones are for."

Charlotte sighed with exhaustion and picked the wall phone off its hook once more. She would try again. But this time, just like the three times before, she only got Sam's voice mail message:

"Sam here. You know the drill. I'll get back to you."

And then the operator's recorded voice informed her to stay on the line to leave a message.

"Sam, er . . ." Charlotte hated talking to machines. "This is Grandma, again, calling at five . . . half past five. Please call home as soon as you can."

She hung up, unable to erase the horrible mental picture of their truck nose-first in a ditch. "Why wouldn't he pick up his phone?" she asked Emily, who should know that sort of thing.

"Either his battery is dead again, he doesn't have it turned on, or there's no coverage. Coverage is so lame around here."

In a couple of minutes, she was going to send Bob and Pete out to search. Only, where?

She heard a door slamming and heavy footsteps coming up the stairway.

"Where's Pete's truck?" rumbled Bob, standing at the top of the steps with his hands on his hips. Charlotte noticed he asked first about the truck, rather than the two boys riding in it. He pushed a worn red baseball cap with a seed company logo back from his forehead. "You didn't tell Sam he could be out joyriding after dark, did you?"

"Of course not!" Charlotte was a little irritated at Bob for suggesting such a thing. "He and Christopher left just after lunch, and they were supposed to come right back after they put up those posters around town, so they could deliver all these pies to Mel's Place."

Emily gestured at the box, loaded and ready to go downstairs. "We've been working on these all afternoon."

"It's not the pies I'm worried about now," said Charlotte.

The phone rang.

"That's Sam!" She snapped it off the cradle before the first ring ended, answering with a breathless hello.

"Me again, Charlotte." Melody's voice came over the line.

"Oh."

"Yeah, sorry to disappoint you, but I really do need those dozen apple-caramel and pumpkin tonight for the Rotary banquet. I promised Gwen we'd have them to her ten minutes ago, and now she's running around putting up decorations and acting skittish. You think you can go ahead and run them out here?"

Charlotte looked at the pies in their box, as ready now as they had been an hour ago. Perhaps they weren't off to a good start after all. But what about the boys? She couldn't just ignore the fact that they could be in trouble somewhere.

"Charlotte? Are you there?"

"Yes, of course. I am so sorry, Melody. The pies are . . . on their way. We'll have them to you in just a few minutes."

"Wonderful! So how's your help working out?"

Just then Emily waved at Charlotte and pointed out the window. She mouthed the words, "They're here!" and Charlotte caught a glimpse of headlights bouncing down the driveway as well.

"Thank you." Charlotte couldn't help breathing her prayerful thanks.

"Pardon?" Melody sounded confused at the gratitude.

"No, no. I mean—never mind. My help is all here. Just a few minor kinks in the system."

"Well, we all have a few kinks, and I know you'll work 'em out, Charlotte. So I'll tell Gwen to go ahead with laying out the main course, and we'll see you in just a few."

Charlotte agreed, hung up the phone, and drafted her husband into service.

"Could you pick it up by that handle, please?" She pointed at the pie carrier. "I need these taken downstairs and put into the backseat of my Ford."

Bob paused for a moment, as if looking for a way out.

"And whatever you do," she added, "don't tip them!"

She didn't wait for an answer, just hurried down the stairs and held the outside door open for him. It wasn't all that heavy, but he hobbled with the awkward carrier down the last step and out into the frosty air, mumbling something about how this wasn't "training them up in the way they should go."

"I thought the boys were going to deliver 'em for you," said Bob.

Charlotte didn't answer him as she hurried across the gravel parking area toward her own little car—just as Sam and Christopher pulled up and crunched to a stop in the gravel. Christopher waved wildly and hopped out his side almost before Sam cut the engine.

"We got totally lost!" announced Christopher. Lost, on the straight shot between Bedford and their farm? They had been traveling the easy back-and-forth road for the past several months with no problems.

"Couldn't help it, Grandma," explained Sam, looking a little more sheepish than Christopher. He plugged at a loose spot of gravel with the toe of his tennis shoe. "There's no signs out there, and Meadowlark turns into something else, and then there's this weird curve that goes off into nowhere, and—"

"Wait a minute," Charlotte interrupted with a raised hand. "What were you doing on Meadowlark? That's the other side of town from here."

"Uh . . . yeah." Sam obviously had something he didn't want to share. "Well, you see, the guy at the tractor parts place said I could deliver stuff for him after school. It would only be a couple hours, and it wouldn't get in the way of what you wanted me to do."

"We were delivering an alternation," volunteered Christopher. He seemed as eager to tell their story as Sam was reticent, but Sam waved him off.

"I can tell her, okay? And it's an *alternator*."

"Loaded and ready." Bob returned from her car and handed her the keys. He gave the truck a curious once-over in the single light from Pete's little porch. "You better get them to Melody before she blows a gasket."

Sam was actually taking another job, just when she needed him the most? She could hardly believe what she was hearing. "That's my job," said Sam, sounding apologetic, but that still didn't explain why he was doing what he was doing. "I can do it."

"Not this time." Charlotte was glad the surrounding dusk hid her face, at least for the most part. Unfortunately, it could not mask the impatient tone of her voice. "I'll do it myself this time."

"But—"

"We'll talk when I get back." She turned and hurried to

her waiting car. "You can explain about the alternator, too, or whatever it was."

She hoped for his sake he had a better explanation. Of all nights to be AWOL, Sam would have to pick their first delivery. Today she would have to be the baker, business-woman, and delivery driver combined. Who was it who said, "If you want the job done right, let a woman do it"?

Thankfully, Pete's measurements had been on the mark when he'd built the pie box; it seemed to have fit snugly through the back-door opening.

"Aren't you going to tell her how much more they're going to pay you?" Christopher's little voice carried across the yard. She froze at the words.

"Shut up," countered Sam. "I told you I'd take care of it."

"You're not supposed to say 'shut up.'"

"Who says?"

"Grandma. You're going to get in trouble."

"Not if you shut up and don't tell her."

Charlotte climbed into her car and started the engine before closing her eyes. *This isn't going the way I'd hoped, God.*

She prayed earnestly for a moment before turning the key again—forgetting that she'd already started the car. The horrible grinding noise jolted her back to the awareness of what she was doing. She heard a *ping-ping* and turned to see her husband knocking on the window.

"Going to shred the starter." He told her the obvious before she'd even rolled the window down.

"Charlotte?" Bob's quiet voice reminded her that she was still sitting in the car with the engine idling. She shifted into reverse.

"I wasn't trying to shred anything," she finally told him.

"Good, but uh, Pete and I were just wondering about dinner. You have any idea?"

"Honey, I—" She sighed and shook her head. If he wanted dinner a little sooner, he could have volunteered to make this delivery for her.

"No hurry." He raised his hands as if in self-defense. "I know you've been working hard on all this pie stuff. It's just that the kids are pretty hungry, too, and—"

"Then you make them something," she blurted out, and instantly regretted it.

"What? Me?" He seemed to take her seriously. "What would I make them?"

"I don't care. Anything. Heat them up a can of chili. There's some in the pantry cupboard. It doesn't matter. I just need to do this. I'll be back by seven."

Twenty minutes there, a few minutes at Melody's, twenty minutes back. That sounded about right. She hated to leave him standing there in the dark, looking more like a lost puppy than her strong husband. They would not see the tears that now blurred her vision, but still she turned her head away from the bickering brothers and steered her car as best she could down the gravel lane. She nearly sideswiped a fencepost at the edge of the property, but hardly cared.

Even though she was on her way to deliver a full load of pies, and even though Emily had helped all afternoon without a complaint, still Charlotte couldn't help feeling as if she had failed completely. Day one of the grand pie-making adventure, and the only thing she wanted to do was cry.

Maybe Bob was right. How was this endeavor going to help their three grandchildren?

She hadn't taught her young charges anything worthwhile. Had she? Well, perhaps she'd made a small amount of progress with Emily. It was more like two steps forward, three steps back. And besides all that, she gathered that her delivery boy had perhaps already defected before he'd made his first delivery, and now she'd allowed her own stubbornness to prevent him from making up for his mistakes. Is that what she and Bob were teaching these kids? One strike and you're out?

She paused at the end of the driveway, resting her forehead on the steering wheel and catching her breath.

I suppose this is why you designed parenting for younger people, Lord.

Finally the aroma of just-baked pumpkin and apple-caramel pies roused her from her worries. But still she couldn't help wondering—

Why did I ever let Hannah and Melody talk me into this mess?

Chapter Thirteen

"Thank you, thank you, thank you." Melody gave Charlotte a big hug once the batch of pies had been offloaded and her banquet room stocked with desserts.

"You're welcome." Charlotte did her best to keep a pleasant face on. "I just hope people will enjoy them."

"Are you kidding? That's not even a question. The only question is, will we have enough for the banquet with enough left over for other customers?"

Charlotte hefted the empty pie carrier, judging if she would be able to lug it back into her car by herself. She couldn't stay long, and the rest of Melody's little restaurant looked busy, even for a Saturday night. Ginny scurried from table to table, her hairnet nearly flying off. And Melody gazed up at Charlotte with a curious expression, bless her heart.

"What's the matter, dear? I hate to say it, but you look like death warmed over."

Leave it to Melody to bring her the plain, unvarnished truth.

"Unfortunately, that's exactly what I feel like." Charlotte looked her friend in the eye, wondering how much she could explain. "I honestly had no idea this work would take so much out of me."

"Now you know how I feel." Melody laughed. "Most every night!"

"Well, I don't mind telling you, I have a brand-new admiration for what you do."

"But you do have good help, right? How's that working out?"

Charlotte wasn't about to launch into all the afternoon's details just now, and certainly not here in the middle of the restaurant for all to hear. She would settle for the condensed version.

"Well, I'm certain they're all learning," she finally said. "It's going to be good for them, as long as I give them a chance."

That seemed to satisfy Melody.

"I just think you're a wonderful grandma for taking this on, and for getting your grandchildren involved."

Charlotte's shoulders drooped when she sighed.

"If only it was that simple, Melody."

Now was obviously not the time to go into this. Melody should be working, and Charlotte had to get home for dinner, besides. She turned to leave, but Melody happily kept the conversation going, even as she wiped down a table.

"There's a play at the middle school tonight," Melody told her, "and I'm thinking we might have even more of a rush afterward, people coming in for dessert."

"You're busy, I'm sure." Charlotte backed toward the door. "But do let me know when you want some more."

"How about another five for tomorrow night?"

"Did you say five? What, are you having another meeting? A Christmas party?"

Melody just grinned as if she had a secret and curled her finger for Charlotte to follow her back through the trim little kitchen. Charlotte waved to the young backup cook, who blew a wisp of hair from her forehead as she juggled several orders on the grill. Walking through the delightful smells of grilled hamburger and chicken, coleslaw, and Melody's famous chowder reminded Charlotte that she'd not eaten anything since a bowl of cornflakes at breakfast. No wonder her knees felt so wobbly and her head so light all of a sudden.

She paused for a moment, leaning against the door of Melody's walk-in freezer.

"Now you really look ill." Melody paused and studied her face. "Are you sure you're all right?"

"Nothing that a good night's sleep won't fix." Charlotte put up as pleasant a face as she could possibly manage, hoping Melody wouldn't call a medic.

Finally, Melody pulled her into her little office in the back, which was hardly bigger than a walk-in closet and filled to the ceiling with boxes, supplies, and kettles.

"Close the door," said Melody, and Charlotte obeyed. "And you'd better sit down."

"Actually, I'm—"

"Sit, girl!" Melody rifled through a foot-high stack of papers on her desk, anchored by a tray of cinnamon rolls.

"Because first of all, you look like you need to take a load off your feet. Second of all, you need to eat one of these rolls. It's a new recipe. And third of all, you're not going to believe this."

As Charlotte gratefully devoured the sweet roll, Melody dug a sheet of paper from the pile and handed it to her with an inscrutable half-smile.

"Is something wrong?" Charlotte asked, savoring the sweet cinnamon tickle on her tongue. This might have been the best cinnamon roll she'd ever tasted.

"Just read it."

So Charlotte squinted at what appeared to be a print-out of an e-mail. She didn't recognize most of the computer-speak at the top, but it did look as if it was dated just yesterday. By holding it at arm's length, she could make out that much. But without her proper glasses . . .

"Cindi Slate of *Cindi's Kitchen.*" She looked up from reading.

Melody nodded. "Well, read it, for goodness' sake! Do you need to borrow my glasses?"

"Actually," Charlotte shifted in the little chair, "I left in such a hurry, well, I didn't think I'd be needing my glasses for anything."

"Here, then." Melody snatched the paper back and read it aloud. "It says here that 'Cindi Slate, well-known host of the KNEB hit show *Cindi's Kitchen,* will be doing a series on Nebraska Hidden Treasures, family recipes from little-known farm communities and their stories.' So she's coming right back here to Bedford."

"You mean she contacted you?"

"Go figure. Somebody told her about Mel's Place when she was here before, and then she found out about our pies, and there was some kind of cancellation for the show she wanted to do in Lincoln . . . I don't know. We're a typical small-town bakery-restaurant, I guess. All I really know is she asked to come tape the program tomorrow afternoon."

"*Tomorrow afternoon?* Such short notice! Didn't you tell her you're not open Sundays?"

"Are you kidding? I am now! Even the Lord said it's okay to rescue your donkey on a Sunday if it falls into a well."

"Actually, I think that was an ox." Charlotte didn't mean to correct her Bible story. Nebraska farmers had a long history of working their farms on the Sabbath, simply because cows still needed milking and pigs needed feeding seven days a week. That wouldn't change.

"Donkey, ox . . . you know what I mean. I'm calling everyone in town to make sure people know about it."

Tomorrow? But Melody just bubbled on with her enthusiastic plans.

"Pie's going to be on the house, by the way. Little sample pieces. That's what I'm telling everybody, and that's what's going to bring people in. Ever been to that big Sam's Club in Grand Island, where they hire all those gals to stand and hand out food samples everywhere? That's what we're doing, my friend. Marketing. That is, if you can bring me a few extra by tomorrow afternoon."

"Oh, dear. I—I just don't know if I can get them to you that soon."

"Sure you can. I'll pay you extra. Just pop a few in the

oven tonight, and a couple more in the morning, and we're all set. You don't have to do any fancy braiding in the crust, the way you've been doing. Just good, old-fashioned country pies. Although, come to think of it, maybe one or two with a nice, pretty crust would be good. What do you think?"

"Well, yes, if there's going to be television cameras. Maybe we should."

But could she get enough help tonight—or even tomorrow—for another full batch of pie baking?

"How many, again?" Charlotte tried to sound upbeat. "Would three extra be okay? Er, four?"

"Oh, dear, no. I was thinking another dozen, if you could."

A dozen? That many?

"Melody, I—"

"I know, I know. Short notice. Make it eight then."

"I still don't—"

"You'll thank me when this is all over. Just think of what Cindi Slate is going to say on her show, sitting here in Mel's Place, lifting a bite of fresh cherry-berry pie to her lips."

"All right." Charlotte took a deep breath as she got to her feet. "I'll make another six. And I'll see you tomorrow afternoon."

"By three in the afternoon, if you can. Cindi and the camera crew are supposed to be here by four to set up." Melody followed her out and back into the kitchen. "You're a dear, do you know that?"

Charlotte wasn't quite certain what she felt like, except

she was certain *dear* did not apply in this case. She tiptoed out past the steaming kettle of chowder and back out to the front room.

"Now don't work too hard, Charlotte," Melody called out after her. "Be sure to have those teenagers of yours help you."

She waved good-bye and escaped to her car. In the process she nearly went sprawling on a patch of ice, grabbing the nearby parking meter for support. Somehow she couldn't help feeling just a bit wicked for what she was about to do.

"I'm sorry, God," she whispered, looking up at the dark gray sky. No moonlight shone through to encourage her, not even a star. Just darkness. "But it looks like I have an ox to rescue tomorrow."

The rescue operation would start that night. When she finally pulled up in front of Pete's dark place, she assumed first that he was over at the house, looking for a meal. She pushed aside thoughts of dinner though.

I should get a couple pies started baking here first, she told herself. *Then I can run over and make sure everyone has something to eat.*

She rapped on the door before poking her head inside and slipping out of the cold.

"Yoo-hoo!" she called up the stairs. "Anybody home? Pete?"

"Grandma?"

"Oh!" Charlotte jumped at the sound of Christopher's voice and whirled to see him standing behind her with a towel-covered tray. Emily and Sam hurried up behind him.

"Didn't mean to scare you," he said.

"We saw your car," said Emily, "and we thought you'd want some dinner."

"Actually, I don't know if I have time." Charlotte recovered enough to lead them up the stairs and into the kitchen.

"You always tell us we need to eat." Emily cleared away several mixing bowls so her brother could set the tray down while Charlotte caught a whiff of something good.

Christopher lifted the larger bowl to reveal a smaller one full of steaming chili flanked by two generous slices of buttered cornbread, celery sticks, and a tall glass of milk.

"If you'll sit down and eat something," said Sam, "we'll help with your next batch of pies."

She didn't question Sam about helping or about his new job. For now, he was here, and helping, and she supposed she couldn't ask for more.

"Oh, kids." She shook her head. "You have no idea how much work we have."

"Yeah, we do," said Emily. "Melody called the house. I think she's calling everybody in the county about the show tomorrow."

Suddenly Charlotte's knees felt quite weak, and she could have started crying all over again. Instead, she lowered herself gratefully into a vinyl-covered kitchen chair and breathed deep.

"Who made the cornbread?" she asked. "And how?"

"I did." Sam stepped forward. "It's an old family recipe."

"Yeah, right!" Emily contradicted him. "The instructions are right there on the box. And Grandpa did most of the work."

"Shut—" Sam started to argue, then apparently thought better of it. Instead, he went to the counter and picked up Charlotte's bowl of pumpkin mix. "You just eat your dinner, Grandma," he told her. "Tell us what to do, and we'll do it."

Charlotte imagined she could do that, after bowing her head to silently thank God for her dinner and the grandkids who had prepared it for her. But she had to know—

"Did your grandfather really help with the cornbread?"

That would be a first. Christopher nodded his head as he rinsed off mixing bowls in the sink he could barely reach.

"And the chili, except I helped with that mostly."

"You worked the can opener," said Emily.

"Nothing wrong with that." Charlotte spread some honey on her cornbread from the little plastic bear container they'd included with the meal. "How about Uncle Pete?"

Emily and Sam looked at each other with a knowing smile. Emily volunteered the latest intelligence.

"He's out on a date with you-know-who," she said. That explained the dark apartment. "Except they didn't call it a date, 'cause there were some other people going too. I think they went to a movie in Harding."

"*Ohh!* Miss Simons." Charlotte couldn't help sharing the little smile that went around the room. But Christopher was the first to bring them back.

"What's so funny?" he asked.

"Wait a couple years," answered his sister, picking up a bowl. "You'll understand."

Charlotte quietly ate her dinner, praying she'd be there to see Christopher go out on a date, for Sam to go to college, for Emily to get married. She prayed for enough time with all of them to make a difference in their lives, for many of the life choices they would be making.

And she prayed for strength to bake six more pies by tomorrow afternoon.

Chapter Fourteen

Fifteen minutes into the next morning's sermon, Bob leaned over to whisper in Charlotte's ear.

"Maybe you should have stayed home," he told her. "You're not here anyway."

"Of course I'm here," she whispered back, trying not to sound defensive.

He just glanced down at the "Sermon Notes" bulletin insert she held in her lap. She moved her hand to cover up the list she'd been doodling. He'd noted that she was running low on shortening, sugar, nuts, and caramel.

I'm sorry, Lord. Feeling as if she had been caught talking by her third grade Sunday school teacher, she sat up straight and renewed her attention on Pastor Evans's sermon.

She was certain it was probably one of his better ones, though for the life of her she could not bring her mind to follow it. A pool of red-and-violet-colored light streamed through the window, slowly making its way across the gray sanctuary carpet. Anita Wilson, who had been attending Bedford Community Church most of her eighty-seven years, could not have imagined the way her finely set hair appeared in bright purples and reds.

Meanwhile, Charlotte found herself calculating how they could be able to finish baking the remaining four pies for the Cindi Slate show this afternoon, and what they would need to meet the deadline. She did the math three times in her head, calculating how long it would take to preheat the ovens and swing into action.

Maybe Bob was right again, she mused. *Maybe I should have stayed home.*

But she couldn't reconcile missing worship for such a thing, no matter how distracted she might have seemed to her husband . . . or anyone else. After all, she had hardly missed a Sunday in ten years. Certainly she needed to be here, even if her mind wouldn't focus. Still, she couldn't help but perk up when Pastor Evans spoke straight at her.

"And by the way, we'll see you all at Melody's in a few hours. Right, Charlotte?"

Charlotte caught her breath, and for a moment wasn't certain if she had just imagined him asking that. But the smiles around her told her it was true, so she smiled and nodded. He'd finished his sermon, and the final hymn took its place.

Four minutes later she was hustling out through the front doors, Bob and the kids in tow. Anita Wilson looked at her and opened her mouth as if she was about to say something, but Charlotte smiled and waved instead, never slowing down.

"Sorry, Anita. Have to run."

Charlotte didn't even stop to change clothes when they returned home. She simply tied on the flour-dusted old apron she'd been using and launched right into the last four pies on her "to bake" list.

"OH DEAR." CHARLOTTE POINTED at a lineup of parked cars. It looked as if everyone from Bedford Community Church and Holy Family Catholic, and even the Pentecostal church, had parked out on the street in the middle of the afternoon.

"What's the traffic jam?" Christopher leaned over the backseat to see what was going on, with more cars downtown than anyone had seen in a while.

"It's for the show," said Emily.

It seemed as if everyone for twenty miles around had decided to come see what was going on at Melody's. Dozens of pickups lined the way in front of them. A large white van with a sizable satellite dish on top and KNEB REPORTS on the side had double-parked in front of the little restaurant, causing even more of a jam.

"No way all these people are getting inside that little restaurant." Sam announced what everyone had to be thinking. Charlotte wondered how long all the people on the street would stick around if they couldn't get a good view of the action.

"Drop us off here, Grandma," suggested Emily. "I see Ashley. We'll run the pies inside."

Charlotte shook her head, but she didn't want to make them later than they already were. If they wanted to make their delivery, she would have to try a more creative approach.

"I'm coming with you," she replied, pulling right up behind the van. If they could double-park, well, so could she. She set the brake and turned on the four-way flashers. "Come on!"

Once outside, they had to wade through the curious crowd, standing elbow-to-elbow on the sidewalk. Dana Simons waved at them from a few yards away, and Emily quickly found her friend Ashley, Melody's daughter. Everyone, it seemed, wanted to catch a glimpse of Cindi Slate up close. How would they ever get through?

Fortunately, she had Sam to heft the box and announce their entrance.

"Pies coming through, people!" he yelled above the buzz of the crowd. "Pie delivery for the show. Make way!"

Charlotte stopped short at the doorway, almost not recognizing what she saw. Mel's Place had been transformed. A number of assistants scurried about as they mounted lights on their stands, reflectors, and two cameras on tripods. Others wired the equipment together, yelling and gesturing to coworkers. Charlotte had no idea what they were doing, only that she had rarely seen such a controlled mass of confusion. Sam found a clear place on the counter to set down their box, right in front of where Melody was standing, watching the setup.

"We had a hard time getting through the crowd," Charlotte explained. Unfortunately, she had to raise her voice to be heard above the buzz.

Melody raised her eyebrows. "But the pies are okay?"

Charlotte nodded and found a place behind the counter to open her box and carefully removed the still-warm pies. They had been bounced around rather a little too roughly, but hopefully they would still photograph well.

"Here we are." She pulled them out with a relieved smile, presenting them to Melody. "One of them is a little bruised, but—"

"Only one?" Melody looked around at her crowds, at the two young ladies directing bright lights at the ceiling, and at a dark-haired man pointing a shoulder-mounted camera at a petite woman sitting alone at a round table set up in the middle of all the action.

"Cool!" said Emily, standing on tiptoe with Ashley to see the focus of all the attention. That, apparently, would be Cindi Slate.

But by this time a particularly agitated young man with longish hair and jeans scurried from the camera to Cindi and back, setting up the shots, demanding more lights, and motioning for people to back away. He parked his hands on his hips, looked around the crowd, and noticed Charlotte.

"You!" He pointed at her without ceremony. "You the pie lady we've been waiting on?"

Charlotte nearly dropped the surviving cherry-berry pie.

"Actually, my grandchildren and I—"

But he wasn't listening as he hurried over to her and draped an arm around her shoulder.

"All right, dear, we're going to have you bring the pies over to Cindi, and she'll give one of them a taste, a few close-ups of the pie, and she'll just ask you a few questions. Do you understand what we're looking for here?"

He didn't wait for an answer, but she jumped when he brushed a finger across her cheek.

"You're not wearing any makeup." He paused, then dug into his pocket for a compact and proceeded to dust her cheeks and forehead. "Hold still then. I usually only have to do this for the men."

She held her breath, trying not to move, and everyone in the room was staring at her by this time. Out of the corner of her eye she noticed Pastor Evans. Finally her makeup man studied his work and nodded.

"It will have to do," he told her, and nodded toward the table. "Now go. We're running behind schedule."

Charlotte looked over at Melody for help, desperately looking for a way out of this horrible fix.

"You didn't tell me anything about this!" Charlotte whispered at her in passing.

"I didn't know!" The proprietor of the little restaurant only shrugged her shoulders. "They just said they were coming and wanted to taste something local. You're local."

Oh yes, she was local, all right. On display, and on stage. And she had no idea what her hair looked like, only that she'd been working in a kitchen all afternoon. At least she still wore her navy blue church dress, though it was splotched here and there with flour prints. What she would have done to be able to fade into the crowd.

Christopher, on the other hand, had worked his way into the front row of spectators and was waving excitedly at her.

"Go, Grandma!"

Go, indeed. Cindi Slate greeted her with a perfect, straight-toothed smile and began chatting with her like an old friend, peppering her with questions.

"After I visited your fairgrounds I heard so much about your recipes, dear. From your grandmother, I hear?"

How did she know to ask? Melody must have told her everything.

"Actually, my husband Bob's mother. She taught them to me when we were just married."

Charlotte hid her shaking hands under the red-checked tablecloth and tried to ignore a microphone on a pole suspended only inches from her face. The host took it from there.

"Well, people in this part of small-town Nebraska are famous for their wonderful country recipes, passed down from generation to generation, hidden away in handwritten cookbooks or brought out only at county fairs and church potlucks."

Cindi smiled into the camera and delicately spooned herself a bite of pie. Charlotte wondered if it might stain the woman's bright white teeth or rub off some of her lipstick, though she was probably wearing the kind they advertised on TV, guaranteed never to come off without a good application of paint thinner.

As the host spoke her eyes bulged and she paused in mid-sentence.

"Oh my." She took the Lord's name in vain and another bite, perhaps to be sure. This bite was considerably less dainty. Charlotte felt herself sweating profusely. Cindi stared at her with open-eyed wonder.

"Dear, what did you put in this?"

"Well, ah." Did she want to hear the recipe right now? "I don't—"

"Certainly you don't. If I'd baked this pie, I wouldn't be telling a soul either." Now Cindi Slate stared directly at the camera and strung her words out for effect. "This—is—the most incredible—piece—of—pie—I—have—ever—eaten. There must be some kind of secret—"

She took yet another bite and chewed for a moment before going on, rolling her eyes and moaning.

"Some kind of special ingredient that I've never tasted before. And this crust! Who would have thought, right here in the middle of nowhere?"

Charlotte had never considered Bedford "nowhere," but she let their guest prattle on about finding wonderful hidden culinary treasures in the most unlikely of places, about getting out and trying new taste adventures, and then about next week's show. The entire taste test had lasted perhaps fifteen minutes, if that.

All this hullabaloo, she wondered, *just for that?*

"From Mel's Diner in the quaint little town of Bedford Falls, I'm Cindi Slate, and this is my world."

She held her smile for a long, unnatural moment before the lights clicked off and the young director descended on them.

"That was great," he told Cindi, pointing to her plate. "I've got to say, you actually looked like you were enjoying that. Good job."

Meanwhile, Cindi had already taken another bite and spoke out of the side of her mouth as she chewed.

"For once, I'm meaning every word of it. I mean—" She looked over at Charlotte as if noticing her for the first time. "Take that as a compliment, dear. This is truly fabulous. I have no idea how many calories, but fabulous."

This time she leaned closer, and in a conspiratorial tone asked for Charlotte's secret recipe, since there obviously had to be one.

"Especially the crust," she added, kissing her fingertips like a French chef. "The flakiest I've ever tasted."

"Well, my mother-in-law taught me," Charlotte explained again, pushing back her chair. "Years ago."

"*Mmm.*" Cindi made her way through yet another bite. "You should package this. Really. I have some friends in New York who would invest in this product tomorrow."

Charlotte stood up as if in a daze. Several of the folks gathered close by began to clap as she made her way back to collect Pete's box and several empty pie tins Melody had gathered.

"That's my pie lady." Melody beamed as she handed

over the stack of tins. "What did I tell you? We're going to be famous."

Charlotte took the tins and handed the box over to Sam, who had been standing nearby with his hands in his pockets.

"Famous is the last thing I want, Melody. I just wanted to sell you some pies."

"Well, hold on to your hat, dear." Melody still stood behind the counter with stars in her eyes. "Because I think things are about to get very interesting."

Chapter Fifteen

By Thursday afternoon, well into what Pete called the "Great Pie Fiasco," Charlotte was beginning to think they were getting the hang of things. Even Bob stood at a distance and admired the pie kitchen assembly line.

"You stay right there," she warned him, shoveling another warm pie from a wooden plate on the counter to the waiting transport box. "I don't want you touching anything. We need to get these pies done, or else."

"Sorry, Grandpa." Christopher scrubbed a pile of cooking bowls and implements in the sudsy sink while Emily mixed fresh ingredients. "Grandma says we've got sanitary conditions here."

"Sanitary, huh?" Bob crossed his arms and stood his ground. "Since when was I considered unsanitary?"

"Since you stepped out of that barnyard, dear." Charlotte closed the lid on a half-dozen cherry-berry and tapped the top of the carrier box. She nodded at Sam, waiting in the living room.

"All set for the Goldenrod Bed and Breakfast," she told him. "You know where that is?"

"Not a clue, Grandma." He picked up the box and started down the stairs. "But if I keep driving and driving, I'm bound to find it eventually."

"What?" she cried. "Wait a minute!"

"Kidding. I know where it is. I just have to drop off a couple parts for Brad first."

"Sam, now wait a minute. I think we need to talk about this. It's just not working to have you do deliveries for Brad and—"

"Sorry, Grandma." Sam was already in motion. "Gotta go."

The door slammed, and Emily slumped her shoulders in disgust.

"He thinks he's so funny," she muttered, gently dropping a lump of fresh dough onto the flour-covered cutting board where she would roll out the next pie crust.

She's learning well, thought Charlotte, appraising her work. Emily worked a little more quickly than she would have liked, but that probably just came with youth. She also talked too fast—sometimes too fast for Charlotte to even understand—but what else was new? Before long Emily would be able to do the entire pie from start to finish.

"You've learned a lot," Charlotte told her, but Emily didn't smile as she whisked aside a strand of blonde hair. Instead, she seemed to concentrate on the rolling and leaned into her work with a sort of grunt. Maybe that was her way of acknowledging a compliment.

"Melody said they've had at least fifteen or twenty families come all the way from Lincoln to the restaurant ever since that TV show aired last Tuesday." She began loading their second transport box with the two remaining cherry-berries. "That's for the VFW party later this afternoon," she told them. She'd just slipped four more in the oven when the phone rang.

"I'll get it!" said Christopher, wiping his soapy hands on a dish towel. He answered the phone with a practiced "Heather Creek Pie Company, home of the world-famous pies featured on *Cindi's Kitchen.* May I help you?"

She would talk to him about the "world-famous" part, and perhaps the rest of his greeting as well. Christopher paused, listening, before his voice fell with disappointment.

"Oh. Sure. She's right here."

He passed the phone over to Charlotte.

"Charlotte, this is crazy, I know." Melody was nearly yelling over all the background noise of a busy restaurant. "But a fellow from Omaha just showed up, saw the TV show like everybody else, and he wants us to gift-wrap pies for all his relatives."

"Omaha? Certainly he didn't come all that way just for pies."

"I know, sounds crazy." Melody's voice lowered, as if she'd covered the phone with her hand. "But that's what he wants, and he's going to wait here until he gets it. He wants pumpkin, by the way. Obviously he heard about how you make them with streusel, and it's something his grandmother used to do. So it's some kind of sentimental journey for him. Says he hasn't heard of anybody doing it with streusel for years."

"Oh!" Charlotte hit her head. "I have four pumpkin sitting here, but Sam just left with a load of cherry-berry. It might be a while. I guess I'll bring them in myself."

"Could you? He seems like a very nice person."

After she hung up the phone, she collected her delivery and briefed her helpers.

"Now, these apple-caramel pies are a special order for the bed and breakfast tonight, so it's important they turn out perfectly. You know when to pull out these four, right?"

Emily rolled her eyes. "You told us a thousand times, Grandma. When the crust is golden but not brown and the apples are blubbling, I mean, bubbling. Another thirty minutes or so. Go ahead. We've got it under control."

Charlotte was about to add a few more instructions but changed her mind. Emily still had a way of getting instantly defensive, and she did seem capable. Okay, then. So she trundled down the stairs and out the door with the pumpkin pies for their man from Omaha.

"Be back in an hour," she called over her shoulder.

A FEW MINUTES LATER Emily leaned out over the sink, catching her breath from dough-rolling and letting warm water run over her hands as she waited for her grandmother's oven full of pies to finish baking. Her mind drifted as she looked across snow-dusted fields between the farm and the road.

Back in San Diego she would have been hanging out with her friends, harassing boys at the mall, and trying to stay out of trouble at school. She thought of her best friend Bekka's fourteenth birthday party last November at South Mission Beach, and how she'd be missing her party this year.

She wanted to call them so bad, but she hadn't been calling as much these days. Even though she liked hanging around with Ashley, it hurt to know that her other friends were there, moving on without her, and she was here.

"Can I ask you a question?" Christopher's little voice broke into her daydreaming.

"Depends."

"Do you think Grandpa and Grandma would ever sell the farm?"

She looked down at him to make sure he was serious.

"Why would you say something like that?"

"I heard Uncle Bill talking about it a while back."

"Uncle Bill says lots of stuff. You probably didn't understand what they were saying."

Christopher crossed his arms, looking unconvinced. But really, what a lame thing to worry about.

"I understood what they were saying," he finally countered. "I'm not stupid."

"I didn't say you were. But if you're that worried about it, why don't you ask Grandpa yourself?"

"Forget it." Christopher didn't look happy with that answer as he came up behind her and leaned up over the sink too. He could barely see through the window, even if he stood on his tiptoes. Still, he must have been able to see enough so that he suddenly pointed and screeched.

"Look out there!" He bounced with excitement as he yelled. "It's Toby!"

Emily followed her brother's wild pointing to see a frantic motion less than a hundred feet away. It didn't look like their dog though. At first it reminded Emily more of a whirling cartoon character, like the coyote fighting with the roadrunner. Something that resembled fur flew in all directions mixed with snow and mud. Whatever it was, Christopher absolutely freaked out.

"She's getting killed!" Christopher grabbed the sleeve of her blouse and tugged, nearly ripping her arm off. She had no choice but to follow him down the stairs and run outside. Besides, she had to see what all the commotion was about too.

By this time though, Christopher was bawling or screaming or both, calling Toby's name over and over almost as loudly as the horrible fight itself. Once outside, there was no mistaking something awful was going on. People all the way to Bedford could probably hear the snarling and barking, and the worst of it was a high-pitched scream like a pig about to die.

Only Toby wasn't fighting with any pig. The ear-splitting racket even caught Uncle Pete's attention, and he ran out of the house to see what was going on.

"Hold on!" Uncle Pete ordered them to a halt, but he had to grab Christopher by the arm to hold him back. Christopher wiggled free and kept going.

"It's killing Toby!" hollered Christopher.

From where Emily stood about ten feet from the fight,

it looked like he was right, and now she could see why Uncle Pete had tried to hold them back. Through the blur of motion and fur, she was pretty sure she could see a raccoon's tail swinging wildly—first on top, then beneath the snarling dog. They stood helplessly by, clapping, whistling and hollering while Toby and the raccoon engaged each other in a fierce, howling battle to the death. It was clear that one of the animals was not going to walk away from this, and Emily had a sinking feeling she knew which one.

"We've got to do something!" yelled Christopher, tears streaming down his cheek. He would have dived into the battle himself had Uncle Pete not held him back by the collar.

"Christopher!" The sharp tone of Uncle Pete's voice made her little brother freeze. For a moment it also seemed to catch Toby's attention long enough for the dog to pause and look over at them.

That's when Christopher broke free and the raccoon disentangled itself to scurry away through the corn stubble.

As quickly as it had started, the fight was over.

Toby, however, appeared to have taken the worst of it, and nearly toppled over before Christopher scooped her up in his arms and the dog wagged her tail weakly.

"Don't touch her, Chris," said Uncle Pete too late. "Hold on for just a second."

"Oh, gross." Emily felt her stomach turn and had to look away, but she'd already seen more than she wanted to: Even in the gathering darkness she could see a horrible gash on the side of the poor dog's face, an ear partly shredded, and who knew how many bites. Christopher just lifted Toby in his arms, and the dog wagged her tail weakly.

"Dumb dog," said Uncle Pete. "Ought to know better than to tangle with a coon."

"She's not dumb," insisted Christopher. "She was just protecting us."

"Well, let's get her back to the barn then. Maybe we can clean her up. But, Chris—" He paused, shaking his head slowly. "Looks like she got good and chewed. She might not make it."

"We have to take her to the vet," Christopher said.

"I don't know if we can do that, sport. She's not livestock, you know."

"What's that supposed to mean?" A new wave of tears coursed down his cheeks. "She's our dog, and we just can't let her die. We have to!"

"Please, Uncle Pete?" Emily couldn't help crying, too, but mostly from seeing her little brother so desperate. Christopher hurried with the dog to Uncle Pete's truck and let himself into the cab.

"Wait a minute, Chris." Uncle Pete held up his hand but gave up with a sigh.

Emily wasn't sure why she rode along in the cab with them to Dr. Trask's office. Mostly she had to be there for Christopher, so she sandwiched herself between her uncle and brother, trying not to touch the injured dog.

Christopher stroked and whispered to Toby the whole way in while the dog whimpered quietly and wagged her tail from time to time. She didn't try to move from

Christopher's arms and probably couldn't. But Emily was afraid Uncle Pete was right, that poor Toby wouldn't make it very much longer. The dog was losing a lot of blood.

"It'll be okay," she told Christopher, and she closed her eyes to pray for her kid brother and his dog.

Please help Toby get through this, she prayed, *for Christopher's sake.*

Fifteen minutes later they pulled up to a trim Victorian house at the edge of town, surrounded by a white picket fence. Light flooded from several front windows while a sign hanging in the front door read Clayton G. Trask, DVM—Large Animal Practice.

Obviously Toby was no large animal like a horse or a cow, but she was large enough to make Christopher stagger as he trundled her up the front steps.

It wasn't until Emily stepped inside that the woozy feeling hit her. Maybe it was the icky smell of antiseptic and injured animals that assaulted her nose and left her head spinning, or maybe the wall poster showing a cross-section of a horse's internal organs. Either way, she was in danger of losing her lunch, and she didn't want to be standing in the middle of the little waiting room-parlor when it happened.

"Do you need to get back outside?" Uncle Pete must have seen the signs. She nodded and made an about-face for the front door.

The fresh, cold air hitting her in the face worked wonders. She gripped the porch railing and took deep breaths, and the butterflies eventually settled back down, one by one. She closed her eyes and smelled damp hay in the distance, felt the hint of frost in the late afternoon air, and wished she had a piece of gum.

That's when she remembered the four apple-caramel pies she'd left baking back in Uncle Pete's kitchen. By now they would be burnt to a crisp, probably filling the building with smoke.

"Oh no!" The memory hit her like a slap in the face. "Oh no!"

Chapter Sixteen

"I told you, Emily, I'm not angry." Later that night Charlotte tossed a stainless steel whisk into a bowl in the sink, adding to the pile of unwashed dishes that threatened to totter over onto the floor. "The bed and breakfast people were very understanding when we brought them some cherry-berry from Melody's."

"But, Grandma—"

"But Grandma nothing. It's after ten, and you have school tomorrow."

"I'm not tired."

"Believe me, you're tired. Your body just hasn't told you yet. Or you're not listening. Now, you just let me finish this up. It wasn't—" She tried not to pause as she did her best to force the words out. "It wasn't your fault, okay?"

The front door slammed, and Pete took the steps two at a time.

"Hey, Mom, you got the fire put out?"

"There never was a fire," she answered, sounding rather defensive. "Everything is under control."

"Oh. Well, that makes me feel better. But that smell!"

"It'll air out." Charlotte waved her apron toward the open kitchen window. Everything still smelled of burned apples and sugar. Strong enough to peel paint, and she didn't blame Pete for holding his nose as he walked by. She had almost fainted herself when she'd rushed into the building a few hours ago.

Now Pete poked his nose into the garbage can under the sink where she had tossed the remains of the ruined pies.

"Woo!" He pulled back with an exaggerated cough. "They look like toasted cow patties. Probably *taste* like—"

"That's enough, Pete. Look, I'm very sorry for the smell, and I do hope you'll be able to sleep. I'll only be a little longer, and I'll be very quiet."

"Oh, don't worry." He smiled. "You know it was my idea to have you use this place in the first place, so I can't complain. We all just had a little excitement tonight too."

She nodded. "Emily told me all about it. I'm glad Toby is going to be okay."

"Probably a good thing we took her to the vet though. Even though Nurse Emily here nearly tossed her cookies when we got there."

"Pete."

"It's okay, Grandma," said Emily. "It's all true."

Maybe true, but certainly unkind. Emily looked as if the afternoon's events were finally starting to catch up to her. Never mind her brave expression; by this time Emily's face had begun to droop and she hugged her arms to her chest, rocking back and forth. She turned to leave.

"I guess I'll go to bed then."

"Tell your brother he can set up a bed for Toby where he

can keep an eye on her," Charlotte said, "if that's what he wants to do. But just for tonight."

"I think he already has."

Emily slipped down the stairs and into the night, leaving Charlotte to her frantic baking. Pete saluted her as he turned to go to bed. He made a show of taking a big breath and sighing deeply.

"Ah," he said, a smile playing at his lips. "Love the smell of napalm in the morning."

"What is that supposed to mean?" She had no idea what he was talking about except that he often seemed to cover up serious times with his silliness and his movie impersonations.

"Never mind, Mom. Don't worry about me. But I've got to get an early start. Dad and I have to stretch some fencing over on . . ."

He trailed off. He must have seen the door open before she did, or felt the blast of cold air.

"Charlotte?" Bob called as he trudged up the stairs. "You still up here?"

She didn't answer. Where else would she be? He stopped at the top of the stairs and stared at her with a wrinkled nose and a curious expression.

"I hate to say it, Charlotte, but I think something went wrong up here. You smell that?"

"It's a new recipe," quipped Pete, before closing the door to his bedroom behind him. "Good night!" Charlotte had heard enough of her son's levity for one night. For that matter, she'd had enough of just about everything from everyone. And she wasn't about to explain the incinerated pies all over again, not to Bob, and not at this late hour.

"I'm sorry, honey," she finally told him. "You go on to bed. I'll be along in a little while."

He didn't answer right away, just crossed his arms and studied her as she returned to her pies. He must have known she had no realistic idea how much longer she would be.

"Is this really what you wanted from this pie business?" he finally asked, and the quiet words stung. They shouldn't have, and she was sure he didn't intend them to, but they did.

"Things happen sometimes." It was a weak answer, and she knew it. But it was all she could manage for now. She kept her voice down so Pete wouldn't hear the back-and-forth. "I just have to deal with it as best I can and get these pies delivered first thing in the morning. Melody's counting on us."

"I know, Charlotte. But . . . *us?* More like, she's counting on *you*. What has this got to do with our verse?"

Our verse would be the one she most definitely did not want him quoting back to her. Please. She knew all too well what Proverbs 22:6 said.

"Nothing to be done about it." She rustled around in a drawer for another spatula, though the one she held was perfectly fine. Bob cleared his throat the way he did on the few occasions he'd stood up to say something in Sunday school. "I thought this was your way to give the kids a job that paid," he said, "for Christmas. Teach them what it means to work, right?"

Charlotte attacked a blob of dough as he went on, probably with too much force, and didn't answer.

"And didn't you say it would be a way to spend more time with them?"

"Bob, you're not being fair."

"I don't think you're teaching them anything by doing it all yourself, and in the middle of the night besides."

He looked over in the direction of Pete's closed bedroom door, obviously sizing up their potential audience. Thankfully he kept his voice down too.

"Look, Charlotte, I'm just worried about *you,* that's all. Not trying to get your goat."

"That's a relief." She hadn't meant the sarcasm that slipped from her mouth, but he didn't seem to notice as he paced the floor at the edge of the kitchen linoleum.

"But you know who didn't do their regular chores this afternoon, nor yesterday either?"

"I—nobody told me about that. I would have spoken to them."

"I already did. Meanwhile, Pete and I both have been running around extra, picking up the pieces."

"Bob, that's not right."

"'Course it's not. Understand, I'm not saying it to complain. But Sam was off driving tractor parts around the countryside, right? And running pies back and forth whenever you ask him? When's he having time to do his regular chores here at the farm?"

"You know I didn't want him to take the second job, Bob. He just wants to earn enough money for a car."

"That much I know. I just want to understand what you think this is teaching them. You haven't told me yet."

By this time Charlotte had produced a paper-thin crust, obviously too thin to be of any use. She peeled it off her cutting board, balled it up, and threw it back into the mixing bowl.

"I can't tell you because I don't know." She turned aside, wiping her eye. As much as she wanted to keep from tearing up, she couldn't. But she went on.

"This hasn't turned out the way I thought, all right? Mostly the kids just bicker, Sam's more distant than ever, and I just end up being short with them. Nights like tonight, it's no wonder. With all this work to do, and not enough time in the day to do it."

He came over and slipped an arm around her, and she buried her face in his strong shoulder without argument. Why did he always have to be so right anyway?

When she breathed in she could almost see the distant fields where he had been working all day, and she let herself enjoy his familiar scent. His shirt was still a bit damp from the cold drizzle outside, but she could have wished he would stay here with her all night. After all, she wasn't going to be able to leave anytime soon.

"Your kitchen inspectors allow me to wash dishes?"

He pulled away and took up station at the sink.

"You don't have to do that," she told him.

"If I ever want my wife back, maybe I do. Guess we'll figure out how to make this program work in the morning. But right now . . ."

He rolled up his sleeves and fished out a bottle of liquid dish detergent from under the sink, then let the hot water kick up a cloud of steam and squirted in three times as much as he needed to.

While Bob started in on her daunting pile of dishes, pie plates, bowls, and utensils, she attacked her pie ingredients once again. With a burst of renewed energy she matched crust to filling, sculpting the scalloped edges of each perfect pie, tasting the filling spices just to be sure.

"You've been so good through all this pie making," she whispered, as much to herself as to her husband.

"What, you mean since I can't have any?" He smiled and shrugged. "You know I manage. But yeah, you're pretty good at tempting me."

She smiled as they worked on in silence, neither having to say a word. Charlotte could tell her husband was trying extra hard to not make the kinds of noises that could wake Pete. He set each item down carefully in the drying rack. And as they continued their work, the clock passed eleven thirty, then midnight, then one. Finally Charlotte pulled the last pie out of the oven with a weak but triumphant smile.

"Presenting the final pie," she said. She didn't bow for fear of toppling over forward. Bob pantomimed silent clapping and rewarded her with a smile of his own.

Who would have thought? Around them, the kitchen gleamed more brightly than ever. Bob had carefully washed and dried each spare pie plate, stacking them neatly in a cupboard above the sink. All the utensils were arranged neatly either in a red plastic vase on the countertop or in a large drawer next to the sink, and the counters had been scoured and wiped down. Flour, sugar, and other ingredients had been stowed with all the other pantry items, almost the way she would have put them away. The state ag inspector would have been proud.

No, the kids hadn't helped or learned any lessons here. She and Bob hadn't trained them in anything, it seemed. But Charlotte felt as if perhaps she was the one who needed to learn this time around. To remember, at least, how much her farmer husband meant to her.

"Does that do it?" asked Bob. If she looked as tired as him, they must have looked like a pretty sorry couple. She didn't want to check in the little hallway mirror at the top of the stairs. Instead she nodded her simple yes and checked that the burner and oven knobs were all in the off position before snapping off the overhead lights.

"Dark in here," she muttered, and followed Bob's blindman's-bluff lead down the stairs, carefully feeling the way with her toes. Once they'd made it down, he slipped an arm around her waist as the sharp night air cut her cheeks.

"Oh!" she gasped, wiping the taste of fine sleet from her face with a sleeve. "That'll wake you up."

"We might as well not even go to bed."

"Ohhh," she groaned. "Please don't say that."

She didn't even want to think of the frightfully abbreviated night's sleep they'd earned, with less than four hours until her alarm would wake them once again. That might work for someone else, but not for Charlotte Stevenson.

Still, she held tightly to her noble husband, doing her best to keep her balance on the newly frozen ground. As they hurried back toward the house a light caught her eye, and she glanced up at Sam's window to see a weak yellow glow. He had either fallen asleep with the light on, or he was staying up far too late.

"Bob." She pointed up in the darkness. "What's he doing?"

Bob might have seen it, but the light immediately flickered out, as if Sam had heard them coming across the yard, or perhaps had seen the light go out in his Uncle Pete's apartment. She couldn't help feeling a bit strange at the thought of Sam awake so late, perhaps keeping track of them in the distance.

"Well, if he's staying up this late," said Bob as he helped her up the steps, "he's going to be dragging in the morning."

Charlotte sighed as they slipped in though their front door and silently pulled off their boots, making as much noise as a burglar.

"Yes, he will," she whispered. "Just like us."

Chapter Seventeen

At first Charlotte thought it might have been a bird tumbling against her kitchen window as she finished the breakfast dishes the next morning.

Funny, she thought, *I don't see any birds*.

A moment later she head the *plink* again, this time unmistakable. But when she looked out she only saw her friend Hannah standing there, bundled against the cold and grinning from ear to ear as she tossed yet another pebble at the window.

Well, that did it. Charlotte returned the smile and hurried to the back door.

"I thought you were a bird!" Charlotte opened the door as Hannah stepped inside.

Hannah stopped just inside the entry, her purple duck boots too wet to wear any farther. "I saw you through the window, so I decided to have a little fun."

"I might have expected that of the kids, but not my good neighbor Hannah Carter." Charlotte had to laugh. "Why don't you just take your boots off and have a cup of coffee?"

"No, actually, I just came over to see if you might want

to take a morning walk." Hannah shifted awkwardly from foot to foot. "It hasn't been much fun walking alone the past week or two."

"Oh, Hannah. I'm so sorry. Has it been that long?"

"I was sick for a while . . ." Hannah shrugged. "And now you're probably busy."

"Well," Charlotte stepped back to the kitchen to replace the dishtowel in her hand, "I have been. But let me just put these dishes away, and I'll grab my coat."

"You might want to wear your earmuffs too." Hannah brightened like a birthday cake whose candles had just been lit. "It's still pretty raw out this morning. But they say we're going to see a little sunshine for a couple of days before the next system comes in."

Charlotte buttoned up her coat and waved at Pete as he emerged from the barn. They started down the driveway.

"I'm going walking with Hannah!" she shouted. They continued down to the road, as they'd done hundreds of times before.

"No canine escort this time?" Hannah looked back to see if Toby would tag along, as she had done so often in the past.

"Actually, no. She's recuperating in the barn. I guess you have some catching up to do."

She started to fill Hannah in on the disasters of the other day, from dog-raccoon conflicts and burned pies to late-night baking sessions and impossible pie deadlines.

"Oh, dear." Hannah walked as far into the narrow shoulder of the road as she could. "I feel responsible. I encouraged you to do this, and—"

A tractor passed them coming the other way, and Walt Freeman waved at them from his place behind the wheel. Charlotte waited for a moment until Hannah could hear her again over the throaty roar.

"No, no, Hannah. You have nothing to apologize for. And besides, I'm sure it's all going to work out. It's just a little bit of a . . ."

A stretch. A strain. The catch in her voice surprised even herself. She honestly hadn't realized tears might sneak up like this just because she was explaining things to a friend. Really, it wouldn't be necessary to cry.

But there on the side of the road, in the midst of miles and miles of fallow Nebraska fields, the emotions of the past couple of weeks all came tumbling down on her with the winds of November.

"I really don't mean to be blubbering about it." Charlotte fought back the tears and rubbed her cold cheeks as if she could turn off the emotions like a frozen spigot.

"Don't be silly." Hannah slipped an arm around her friend's shoulder and let Charlotte cry. "If it was me, I probably would have locked myself in my room with a box of chocolates and some *I Love Lucy* reruns. I would have gone crazy a long time ago."

"How do you know I haven't already done that?" Charlotte managed a smile, though she was half serious about the question.

Who would be crazy enough to take on three grandchildren at her age—and expect to succeed where she had failed so miserably once before?

Hannah listened politely as Charlotte went on, never

interrupting. But a crow flying low and overhead seemed to echo the accusations that had rattled about in Charlotte's head:

You have no business trying to raise these children.

You've already crashed and burned enough for one lifetime.

What are you thinking?

"It's the first thing I think about when I get up in the morning," Charlotte continued. "And the last thing before I sleep. What can I do to help Emily adjust? Is Sam in trouble? Will Christopher make a friend?"

"Because you care." Hannah smiled. "That's normal."

"Nothing I do seems normal anymore."

Charlotte thought back through her daily routine, from the moment the clock radio snapped on with the grain price report at 5:30 AM and Bob rolled out to his chores, the same way he had for decades.

She would turn back the sheets and follow him into the day, through their meals and devotions, their chores and their friends.

Funny, she thought, how routines seemed to lend a lukewarm feeling of sameness, a thin assurance that because this morning was exactly like the last morning, perhaps the day to come would offer the same courtesy. If she could only dress this day in the same routine, perhaps God would oblige them with another twenty-four hours of *safe*.

"I just can't help it," she finally told Hannah. "I feel like I went into this with noble intentions. We wanted to do the right thing, and certainly what God would have us do."

"There. See? I can't see the fault in that."

The kids, though, had tipped her comfortable routine on its head. Perhaps she hadn't realized how tightly she had been holding on to that routine.

If she was honest, now she could see deep fingernail marks inscribed all the way across her days, leading straight back to the first moment Sam, Emily, and Christopher had arrived at Heather Creek Farm. She shook her head.

"Well, no, we were sincere about all this. Maybe a little naïve, but definitely sincere. But I've found that doesn't always count for much, and now everything I thought would happen just seems to have slipped out of my fingers."

"Give me one example."

"Well, everything we've wanted to teach them in this little pie venture has backfired."

Over the next little rise they would be coming upon the Freemans' place. Hannah seemed to have an answer for every doubt.

"Oh, I don't know if you can say that, Char. The kids are helping you, aren't they? It sounds as if they're learning more about pulling together, working toward a common goal. That's something."

"Not quite." Charlotte shook her head again. "They argue more than not. Christopher finds a way to make the other two annoyed at him, bless his heart. He is a little bugger sometimes. Then I find myself getting short with them. They have other things they would rather do, and they're not even doing their everyday chores. It's a big mess. Even Bob can see that."

"So this is way beyond pies, isn't it?"

As always, Hannah had a way of drilling to the point of things when Charlotte couldn't see it.

"You know the pie thing was just my way of trying to build a bridge to the kids."

"And what's wrong with that?"

"What's wrong is they're still grieving, Hannah, and I don't know how to fix it."

"Dear, I hate to tell you this, but it's not up to you to fix anything. Don't you think that's God's job?"

"Well, yes, but what I mean is, they've been with us what, seven months? I've lost count. But Sam still seems as if he's a prisoner looking for his chance to escape. Plus he's running himself ragged making deliveries for Brad Weber and then running pies into town for me, but he insists he can handle it. I'm still not so sure."

Charlotte went on. "Emily—it scares me how much she's like her mother. And now she's on a mission to change the way her school eats. I don't think she's making many friends in the process."

"And Christopher?"

"Christopher." She bit her lip. "He comes home every day, looks for Toby or the cat, and then he just follows Sam and Emily everywhere they go, like a puppy dog himself. He has a good heart, and he's even been tutoring another boy at school. But something is bothering him, and he needs real friends of his own."

"Hmm. Well, I thought the pie business was a good idea, Charlotte, or I wouldn't have tried to talk you into it. But now . . ."

They walked along in silence as the sun made a good-faith effort at an appearance. The fields around the Freeman farm wrapped them in silence, an ill-fitting cloak that only made Charlotte shiver. She listened for signs of life but heard no birds, no cows, no farm equipment. Only a hushed, cold wind that rustled bits and pieces of spent cornstalks along the road and tumbled them into the muddy fields.

"I don't want you to feel sorry, Hannah. It was a good idea, and maybe it still is. I'm down, yes, but somehow, maybe . . ." She decided to say what she did not entirely feel. Didn't feelings follow commitment? "Perhaps God will salvage the mess I've made."

A nondescript brown truck went by trailing acrid diesel smoke and dropping an accidental offering of silage along the way. Bits of dried, shredded cornstalks swirled around their ankles in eddies.

"One good thing." Hannah punctuated the thought with her index finger held high. "The kids will be making a little extra money for Christmas. That was one of your goals with this whole adventure, right?"

Hannah the eternal optimist. God bless her.

"I suppose." Charlotte sighed her reluctant agreement. "We *are* making a little money with all these blessed pies going out the door. And there's more orders all the time."

"There. See?" Hannah brightened.

"Problem is, I honestly don't know how the kids are going to be spending their wages, or if it's just going to be all on themselves. I'm taking Emily and Christopher to the bank this afternoon to open accounts though. Maybe—"

"Maybe you should just consider it another chance to help them see things the way you and Bob do."

"Now there's a scary thought, Hannah. You don't know what you just said."

Even so, Charlotte smiled as they crossed the road and turned to go back. Maybe Hannah was right.

She looked up at the sliver of sun, and it seemed to brighten . . . just a bit.

Chapter Eighteen

"Come up here, honey." Charlotte motioned for Emily to join her and Christopher at the banker's desk the following Monday afternoon. Emily sidled up as if it hurt very much to be seen in public with her grandmother and little brother, but at least she came.

"So this is Emily." Beverly Davidson flashed a brilliant white smile from across her tidy desk and tented her nicely manicured fingertips. Charlotte caught the faint scent of expensive department-store perfume. "I hear you're making quite an impression with the school board."

For a moment Emily looked as if she had no idea what Mrs. Davidson was talking about.

"Mrs. Davidson's husband is on the board." Charlotte did her best to explain.

"Yes, of course. I'm sorry." Beverly backed up. "I was referring to your menu suggestion at the school cafeteria. I think it's a lovely idea. I've always thought the school should offer more healthy choices."

"Oh. Right." Emily nodded, still looking unsure. After a pregnant pause, Beverly cleared her throat and directed their attention back to the paperwork.

"Yes, well, as I was telling your grandmother, you'll be able to access the account by yourself in the future. There's really nothing to it."

"What about Sam?" Christopher asked. "How come he doesn't have to do this, and just us?"

Charlotte sighed and felt that all-too-familiar impatience rising inside. She smiled and intentionally stilled her voice.

"Sam is running deliveries for Mr. Weber this afternoon, but he promised he would come in himself and take care of it as soon as he was done."

Christopher frowned, but he listened as Mrs. Davidson went on to explain the process of deposits, withdrawals, passbook accounts, interest rates, and signature cards. When she had finished, she leaned back in her chair, held her chin like a professor evaluating her students, and cocked her head to the side.

"Now," she asked, "did you understand all that?"

"I didn't get what you meant about being interesting." Christopher wrinkled his nose.

"Interesting?" Mrs. Davidson was puzzled by his question until Charlotte interpreted for her.

"I think he meant interest. And I don't think they've covered percentages yet in the fifth grade."

"Oh, percents?" Christopher perked back up. "Why didn't you say so? I've been trying to explain that to Dylan at school, but he doesn't get it. I know percents. Like five percent and twenty percent and ten percent. That's easy."

"Well." Mrs. Davidson straightened in her chair and brushed a speck of lint from her expensive plum-colored business suit. "I'm impressed, and I'm glad you understand. So would you like to deposit all your pie earnings today?"

Emily fingered the bulging envelope she'd brought, her portion of the cash from Melody's latest payouts. Charlotte could only imagine a struggle being waged inside the young girl's head. But without a word Emily nodded and placed it on the desk in front of her. A moment later, Christopher followed his big sister's example with his own envelope.

"Minus ten percent, right?" Charlotte added. "That's what we set aside for offering, remember."

They both looked at her like she was crazy.

"Ten?" Emily let her mouth hang open a bit to emphasize her astonished question. "You're joking, right?"

"I'm completely serious. We put aside the *first* tenth as our offering. It belongs to God. Well, naturally it *all* belongs to God, so you could give more. Ten percent is just a starting point."

"I thought it belonged to me," Emily whispered.

Her words made Charlotte realize how far they still had to go. No better time though to get them used to the idea of tithing than right here and now, when they were talking about savings, and money, and percentages—and right here in the bank, no less. Perhaps it would have been better if Mrs. Davidson hadn't been there to hear it all, but she attended First Baptist in town, so she would at least understand what Charlotte was trying to say.

"I have twenty-seven dollars and twelve cents," declared Christopher. "How much is ten percent?"

Though he seemed to understand the concept well enough, he still needed a little practice in mental math. Emily, however, did not.

"Take out two dollars, seventy-one cents." She glumly offered the total. "And two-tenths of a cent. Don't forget that. You might go to hell if you forget to give those two-tenths of a cent."

Mrs. Davidson nearly choked on her coffee, and Charlotte reached over to take hold of Emily's knee in a firm, surprised gesture.

"That's not the case at all, Emily." She felt her own color rising now in her cheeks, but no matter who was listening she could not let this go. "Going to heaven does not depend on what you leave in the offering plate."

Emily shrugged a wordless response, and Charlotte began to regret bringing up tithing in the first place, especially here in the bank. Now it was too late to retreat.

I forced the issue, she realized, *and see what happens.* Hadn't Emily's mother reacted precisely the same way to these kinds of things? With sarcastic humor and a sharp tongue, her two weapons of choice. In so many ways, Charlotte was again reminded that Emily was Denise's daughter.

"How did you figure out the two-tenths of a cent?" asked Christopher. "That was cool."

Leave it to Christopher to pick up on the most trivial angle of this exchange. And while Charlotte appreciated the chance to lighten the tone, Emily again beat her to the reply.

"Sixth-grade math," she answered. "You'll learn it next

year. Oh, but I forgot. Here in Bedford they don't study that kind of thing until high school if you're lucky."

Well, that pretty much wrapped up the meeting, didn't it? Mrs. Davidson obviously didn't know how to respond to Emily either, so she simply smiled and extended the rest of the paperwork for them to sign. Emily complied without another word, nearly punching her pen through the paper, and Christopher again followed her lead. He puzzled over his signature a little longer, inventing strokes as he went.

Charlotte was relieved, however, to see Christopher dig out three dollar bills from his deposit and stuff them in his pocket before he scribbled out the total on the face of his cash envelope.

"Seven take away three—" he mumbled to himself as he wrote in a new set of numbers, then turned around the envelope and pushed it toward Mrs. Davidson with a smile of accomplishment. "There. Twenty-four dollars and twelve cents. And no tenths."

By this time Charlotte was quite done with the lecture phase, but Christopher apparently had something else to say to his sister.

"I don't think I'm going to bother with the two-tenths of a cent stuff, Emily. And I don't think God would get mad at me for that kind of thing anyway." He again dug out the three wrinkled dollar bills and held them up at her. "I'm going to give him a tip."

Charlotte exchanged an amused look with Bev Davidson, and the banker politely covered her mouth to cough.

"I'm so glad you came to visit us today," she told them as they all stood to go. Emily managed to return a forced smile, though only briefly. It soured into her usual frown when she turned to go.

"Thank you, Beverly." Charlotte took the other woman's hand, and they watched the children hurry toward the exit. "I'm sorry for— I mean, you handled that very well."

"Not at all. They're just kids, and I know they'll learn. You and Bob are doing a wonderful thing."

On days like today Charlotte honestly wasn't sure how wonderful it was. But if Christopher had just learned about "tipping" God, well, she supposed that was a start. She couldn't be sure, however, if their older brother would actually follow through on his pledge to open an account.

"You'll keep an eye out for Sam, won't you?" she asked.

"Don't you worry about a thing." Beverly walked her to the door. "We'll take care of him."

If he makes it here, thought Charlotte.

Chapter Nineteen

Justin Taylor could pretty much do anything he wanted in the hallways at Bedford Primary, especially when none of the teachers were watching, like now on this ordinary Thursday morning. People laughed when he pretended he was Miss Rivkin and one of the other kids was misbehaving. But that didn't mean he could get away with this.

Christopher saw it coming from the opposite direction, as Dylan Lonetree walked toward him in the hall and Justin followed along just a couple of steps behind. Like a mirror image, every time Dylan twitched, so did Justin.

Kids on either side turned their heads to watch. Some giggled along while others looked up and down the hall—probably to see what had happened to the nearest teacher. The worst part was, Dylan didn't seem to have a clue. So Christopher planted his feet and decided he wasn't going to let Justin by.

"Hey, Chris." Dylan brightened when he finally noticed his study partner. Christopher was still trying to decide how to best handle this without starting a fight in the hallway. He stepped forward and directly between the two, coming face-to-face with Justin.

"Quit it." Christopher crossed his arms for good measure, but Justin played dumb as a teacher hurried by.

"Quit what?" said the bigger boy. "I was just going to lunch."

With a laugh Justin simply brushed by him, bumping him hard with his shoulder and acting as if nothing had happened. He got in a couple more laughs with several more twitches. At least he was gone though. Christopher couldn't help closing his eyes for a second and shivering.

"Thanks," Dylan told him before they began walking again, avoiding the cafeteria for now.

"Did you know what he was doing?" asked Christopher, and Dylan frowned.

"Sure I knew. It's not like he was the first one to ever do that."

They finally stopped by the double doors to the cafeteria, where Christopher dug the toe of his sneaker into the floor behind him, wondering what to do next. They both knew who waited inside. Dylan crossed his arms and shifted back and forth, and finally Christopher decided for both of them.

"I'm not hungry, either," he said. "Maybe we can just share my sack lunch."

"Yeah?" Dylan's face brightened.

"Sure. And, uh, why don't you just ride the bus home with me today? I'll show you my grandparents' farm, we can drive some tractors around, and you can have all the pie you want."

Actually, Christopher wasn't sure how he would manage "all the pie you want," and he sort of wished he hadn't mentioned the tractor part, but it had obviously impressed Dylan, and it wouldn't sound good to back off the offer. So he let it stand, and they split his PB&J sandwich standing out in the hallway.

Only three more hours until school was out. And if they could avoid big bad Justin between now and then, all the better.

"COOL." DYLAN VOICED his approval as they sat in Christopher's room after school. Somehow they'd slipped into the house without attracting Grandma's attention. She must have really been into her baking that afternoon. That's all she did lately.

He knew she would come looking for him soon if he didn't report for duty with Emily and Sam, but they had a few minutes maybe. He pulled out another magazine and folded it back to the front-page ad with the model airplane, a sleek P-51 Mustang.

"This is actually the one I'm going to get." Christopher pointed to the ad, and he knew Dylan would have to notice the impressive price tag.

"You're just going to buy it for yourself?"

"Sure. I'm making tons of money helping with the pie business. Plus I'm going to have money left over for

Christmas. I'm going to get a weather station and this. I might even get my brother something if he's not a jerk."

Speaking of Sam, Christopher had to show his guest what Sam's bedroom looked like, with all the car posters on the wall. Sam would have killed him if he caught them snooping around his stuff, but Sam wasn't there at the moment, was he?

"He's going to buy a car with all his pie money," explained Christopher. "And then we can drive back to San Diego anytime we want. Plus my grandpa is going to sell this farm anyway, so it doesn't matter."

"You still think he is?" asked Dylan.

Christopher shrugged.

"My Uncle Bill comes over sometimes and they talk, or they have like these secret meetings where nobody else can hear. But I know what they're saying. He's going to get rid of this place. Maybe he's even going to sell us with it."

They both laughed at that, though the weird thought of being sold with the farm made Christopher shiver. Wouldn't that be like slaves, like they'd read about in social studies the other day? His grandfather couldn't do that.

Even so, thinking about it made him feel bad, like the way he'd felt when Grandma and Grandpa had first come to get them in San Diego, and they made him and Emily and Sam go to their mother's funeral.

He glanced down at a half-open desk drawer and couldn't help opening it up just a little more.

"Check out all those twenties," said Dylan. He'd noticed too.

"He's been selling some of his CD collection on eBay," explained Christopher. But footsteps coming up the stairway told him to bail out of there, and quickly. He grabbed Dylan's arm, but too late.

"Hey!" Sam blocked their way at the door, hands on his hips. "What are you two twerps doing in here?"

"Don't call me a twerp," said Christopher. "And I'm just showing him the car you're going to buy."

He knew a few strategies for escaping the wrath of his older brother.

"Yeah." Dylan caught on quickly. "Looks pretty cool."

Sam softened a bit and lowered his guard.

"Did you see the one with the Corvette?"

Yes, they had, but Christopher knew they had only a few minutes left until he was trapped in the pie kitchen for the afternoon, and all his other chores loomed as well, so he beckoned for Dylan to follow, and they hurried past Sam down the stairs.

"Hey!" Sam called after him. "Grandma's looking for you."

Christopher had already slipped down the stairs and through the kitchen. He flattened himself against the wall, just inside the back door, signaled with one finger to his lips and pointed for Dylan to follow with the other. Dylan nodded, ready for the game.

Silently they dashed out the door, then from tree to tree until they rolled into the barn. They kneeled in the shadows, catching their breath.

"Did anybody see us?" Dylan didn't mind playing along.

And in the half-dark of the barn's shadows his jerky movements weren't as obvious.

"I don't think so." Christopher listened but heard nothing except the distant cooing of pigeons in the rafters and Trudy, their milk cow, shuffling around. Meanwhile, Dylan had already wandered off to the back of the barn.

"Hey, Dylan!" Christopher ran off to recapture his guest. He caught up with him on the far side, where Grandpa and Uncle Pete kept their old tractor parts and where a workbench was littered with other parts and tools. Dylan had already climbed up on the seat of a rusty old tractor.

"Cool." Dylan worked the steering wheel back and forth. "You know how to drive it, don't you?"

"Sure. If I wanted to." Christopher recalled his promise to Dylan, earlier that day, that they would be able to drive tractors around. Maybe Dylan would be good with just starting it up. Since Grandpa and Uncle Pete didn't seem to be anywhere near, maybe it wouldn't hurt just to try. He probably wouldn't get it started anyway.

So he hoisted himself up to the seat next to Dylan and acted like an expert.

"It's a 1949 Farmall Model H." He recalled what Uncle Pete had told him. "So it was built like before the Civil War, or close. It actually still runs, sort of."

Dylan followed the story, acting duly impressed, while Christopher tried to remember the right order for which buttons to push. He looked around the barn once more, just to be sure they were alone.

"All you have to do to start it is pull this kill switch," he said, "and push the starter button. My Uncle Pete said he used to drive this thing when he was my age. It should start right—"

He must have remembered correctly, because the ancient tractor sputtered and roared to life in a cloud of smoke. Only problem was, it also jolted to life, nearly throwing the two of them off their perches.

"Hey!" yelled Dylan, grabbing Christopher around the neck. "Where are we going?"

Christopher had just enough time to look up and see them hit the back door of the barn, which popped open with a splintering crash and a protesting squeak of hinges. A moment later they were outside and behind the barn, the tractor engine popping and wheezing.

"We're—" Christopher answered, grabbing the steering wheel and wrestling it around. "We're just going on a little spin around in back of the barn here."

Now it was too late for anything else. He would shut it off just as soon as he figured out how.

"Cool!" Dylan found his place on the side, hanging on for dear life. But he grinned from ear to ear, and Christopher couldn't admit that he hadn't meant to take them outside. He also couldn't think of what Grandpa would do if he found out what they were doing. Maybe they would just take it in a tight circle behind the barn, where no one could see them, then head it back into the barn. Grandpa would never know.

The only problem was, by this time they were both having too much fun to just turn around right away.

"Over there!" Dylan pointed for a couple of trees in the distance, just beyond a fence. "Take it 'round the trees!"

Christopher looked over his shoulder and wondered if Grandma would be hearing the tractor by now, or if she would even know who was driving it. If she couldn't see, why would she think anything of it? He decided to take a chance, and steered for the trees.

"This is the coolest ride!" Dylan shouted over the popping of the mighty little engine, and Christopher was inclined to agree. Now he stood up and felt himself the captain of a mighty steamship, heading across the ocean for China, and for miles all he could see was wave and whitecap, not corn stubble or small patches of unmelted snow. When he breathed deep he could smell distant fields of tea mixed with the familiar briny salt of the ocean.

"Full steam ahead!" he commanded their ship. The engine sputtered along, and soon they raced and bumped across the field, halfway to the South Seas. Only a tiny island of coconut palm trees rose up in the looming darkness.

Soon they would have to steer by the stars, and Christopher looked up to see the first evening star peeking out from a dark canopy overhead, earlier than he'd yet seen it. Now he knew which way to steer their craft.

But without warning their small front tires dipped into a dark hole, wrenching the steering wheel from Christopher's tenuous control and launching him head over heels into the air.

He heard Dylan scream, and he himself hit the dark ground with a sickening thud that wrenched his shoulder and knocked the air out of his lungs.

Chapter Twenty

Charlotte checked her wristwatch once more. Hadn't she specifically asked the kids to check in with her as soon as they got home from school that afternoon? She'd been busy mixing several batches of cherry-blueberry filling, and for the first time, she'd missed Christopher's bus when it pulled up in front of the farm. Perhaps she'd been too preoccupied with the baking, trying to fill another big order from Mel's Place. With only a week to go before Thanksgiving, demand hadn't slackened for a moment.

Sam had to make a parts delivery and was going to come home and take Pete's truck.

But why hadn't Christopher stopped by the kitchen yet? And what was that sound? It didn't sound exactly like Pete's engine.

Christopher is probably just playing with the dog, she told herself. *Or maybe Lightning.*

But when she stepped across the tiny living room to look out over the gravel courtyard, she saw the still-bandaged Toby shuffling slowly toward the main house, minus her human friend. The cat was nowhere to be seen. That was unusual, unless for some reason Christopher hadn't yet arrived home, and if he hadn't, well, that was something else to worry about.

She tossed her hand towel aside and stepped down the stairs, and the worry started to rise.

"Christopher!" She called his name even before leaving the building. But when she reached the bottom, Sam nearly bowled her over.

"Grandma!" he shouted, out of breath, yanking the doorknob out of her hand. "You've got to come quick! Christopher and his friend crashed a tractor into a ditch!"

"What?!"

It took a moment for Charlotte to find out that yes, Christopher was okay, but his friend Dylan was apparently trapped under the tractor, that Emily was already calling 911, and that nobody knew where Grandpa or Uncle Pete were exactly, except that they had run into town on some errand over an hour ago.

"You're sure help is on its way?" she asked, running out into the growing gloom of the late afternoon. Panic clawed at her heart.

"I called!" Emily ran out to meet them, and they both followed Sam as he sprinted around the side of the barn. "They said they'll be here in just a few minutes, and they told me to stay on the line."

"Well, did you do what they said?" Charlotte realized too late what she was asking, considering that Emily ran next to them.

"I had to come get you instead," answered Emily, her voice cracking with emotion.

This can't be happening! Charlotte's mind raced at the possibilities, and her imagination only served up the grimmest of options. Was Christopher really okay? And what had happened to his friend?

She ran as she had never run before, keeping up with Sam, following a deep set of tire tracks through the muddy field directly behind the barn, straight for the gully where Heather Creek meandered close to the property.

"I heard the tractor start up," explained Sam, "and I knew Uncle Pete and Grandpa weren't around, so . . ."

She should have brought a flashlight, she thought as she tripped on a tire track and nearly ended up face-first in the wet ground. But she paid it no mind, scrambled to her feet, and hurried to the place where she heard Christopher screaming for help. She prayed the entire way.

"Oh no," she whispered over and over, following the tracks of the tractor wheels right to the deep-set gully, where they disappeared over the edge. Even now she could see the silent tractor on its side at the bottom of the gully, about ten feet below, and her grandson kneeling in the slush and mud.

"Christopher!" she cried. She tumbled down the gully, reaching and clawing her way. A moment later she crawled to his side and embraced him. "Are you all right?"

He gestured toward the wreck, which appeared to be Bob's older Farmall tractor. It lay roughly upside-down, partially hidden in the water, its front wheels twisted grotesquely to the side.

A moment later she realized he was saying, "It's all my fault" over and over. And like Sam and Emily beside him, his attention was focused on the tractor.

Or rather, what was trapped underneath the tractor. Sam finally explained what they all saw.

"It's the Lonetree kid!" he told them, pointing to a muddy sneaker sticking out from under twisted metal. Charlotte would never have guessed it belonged to a little boy if Sam had not pointed it out. "He had his head above the water for a few minutes, but now—"

The poor boy lay pinned under thousands of pounds of tractor, and under eighteen inches of cruel, cold water. Just on the other side of the wreck, Heather Creek gurgled innocently along, concealing her worst fears.

"You saw his face?" she asked.

"For a while." Sam shook his own pale face while Christopher and Emily sobbed in each other's arms. All she could do was step into the icy waters and, using the front of the tractor for balance, pull herself around to the opposite side.

She caught her breath as needles of cold stabbed her feet and ankles, instantly numbing her legs up to her knees. She would not be able to stand here for long.

"He's been under for a couple of minutes, Grandma." Sam's sober pronouncement chilled her even more than the breathtaking numbness of the waters. But she knew she would not give in so easily, though she could see nothing under the roiling surface that now flowed past the twisted tractor. She thought she smelled an acrid hint of gasoline.

They could not wait for rescuers to arrive. If they were going to save this little boy, they could not wait another minute. With everything in her, she knew it—as if God himself was telling her what to do.

"Sam, Emily!" she barked, and the commanding sound of her voice surprised even her. "Over here, now!"

She leaned her shoulder against the side of the tractor, testing to see how far it might move. It teetered slightly, as if caught on a rock. Perhaps that would be in their favor.

"We're going to tip it as far as we can," she announced, breathless. "Do you hear me? We're going to push it to the side so Christopher can pull him out."

By this time she could no longer feel her feet and legs, but she willed herself not to notice. Sam and Emily offered no protest, only splashed into the creek beside her. "I hear you, Grandma." Emily squeezed up next to her, bracing herself for the effort. Charlotte didn't even take the time to think how insane her words must have sounded as they faced the dark hulk of the twisted tractor. Under normal circumstances, she would obviously never even consider such a thing. But these were no normal circumstances.

Sam joined them, three weak shoulders against a ton or more of metal. What else could they do? Stand and watch the poor boy's foot from the safety of the dry shore?

"Lord, give us strength," Charlotte prayed aloud as they leaned against the tractor. She hoped against hope that she would not make matters worse and that they would not crush the little boy. But she couldn't imagine what could be worse than drowning in eighteen inches of water, pinned under the sheer weight of this tractor. She felt her arms and legs tremble as she directed their pushing.

"More!" she shouted. "Christopher! Come here and feel for his hands. You need to pull him out when we move the tractor out of the way!"

They found their footing in the rocky streambed. They pushed and grunted, moving more with each effort. Emily wept openly. Christopher pushed past them and reached down into the cold water.

"I feel him!" he yelled, kneeling in water that washed around his waist. Charlotte knew the insanity of what she asked of her grandchildren, knew the danger of it, but could do nothing else. She had no idea if their rescuers would arrive in five minutes or fifteen. Either would be too late.

"We can't do it, Grandma!" cried Emily. Sam grunted but said nothing. Charlotte prayed one last time.

"On three," she said. "Push like you've never pushed in your life! One . . ." She heard something crack in her own shoulder but ignored it. Nothing else mattered now. "Two, THREE!"

Charlotte might have screamed just as loudly as the other two; she really didn't recall. All she could feel was the tractor rocking up slowly and tipping to the side with a groan of metal. Christopher reached in and pulled.

"I've got him!" he shouted, thrashing about in the water. Christopher tugged and struggled and finally emerged from the creek with the lifeless body of a little boy, looking blue even in the shadows of the late afternoon. Dragging his friend, he headed back around the tractor toward the shore.

Charlotte's body trembled, the tractor shook with its own weight, and she motioned for the other two to move away.

"Now!" she cried, jerking her head to the side. The tractor swayed and groaned and started back down toward them. "Let go! Stay away!"

The tractor plopped back into its awkward, upside-down position in the mud and rocks while she scrambled to her feet and gathered Sam and Emily into her arms. A bright light in her face made her blink, and as she held her grandchildren she realized someone was standing on the bank ten feet above, shining a flashlight at them.

"Down here," she shouted, and that was all she could manage. Her voice had left her, just as surely as the remaining strength in her arms and legs had flowed away with the black waters of Heather Creek. What had she just done? Now the only thing that kept her from collapsing back into the creek was Sam's arm around her waist.

"Mrs. Stevenson!" a voice boomed from above, and now red-and-blue emergency flashers filled the gloom as well. She heard the roar of a truck. Where were Bob and Pete in all this? Emergency radios crackled with the sound of urgent voices, sounding very far away.

On the near shore, Christopher had collapsed with his friend, or perhaps the body of his friend, while several bright white floodlights swiveled to illuminate them as two men clad in firefighter's gear scrambled down to help.

A moment later she allowed strong hands to pick her up and carry her to shore.

Chapter Twenty-One

Christopher knew he was trapped inside a nightmare and that he would wake up soon. He had to. But when he tried squeezing his head between his hands and even pinching himself in the arm, nothing happened. Nothing seemed to work.

Still the ambulance siren blared when they came to intersections, and still he had to hold a handgrip to keep from falling over. His head felt light, and he couldn't stop shivering, even under the blankets the paramedic guys had given him.

Worst of all, he couldn't keep from seeing Dylan's body laid out on a stretcher right in front of him. And it was all his fault.

I shouldn't have been messing around on the tractor.

I should never have started it up.

I should never have driven it outside.

I should never have tried to show Dylan that I could do it.

Christopher hid his face from the nightmare once again, hot tears clouding his vision. He didn't need eyes to see the horrible twisting and turning of the tractor over and over again. He couldn't stop the memory from playing and replaying in his mind.

At first everything had been cool as Christopher pulled out the throttle as far as it would go and their tractor had chugged happily through the fields. Well, it sure made a lot of noise, but that was the point, wasn't it? As long as Grandpa or Uncle Pete didn't hear. Christopher remembered laughing when Dylan stood up and waved his hands around, yelling, "I'm the king of the world!"

That was before they'd tipped over the edge of the gully, and neither of them had seen it coming.

I knew it was there, he accused himself as the memory of falling over and over made him wince and pull back again under his blanket as the ambulance lurched over a gravel road. *I should never have let it happen.*

Either that, or God could have kept Dylan from getting hurt. Maybe killed. The thought made Christopher shiver even more.

"It's not fair, God!" He mouthed the words, not sure if it counted as a prayer. But still he had to say it, just for the record. "Dylan didn't do anything wrong. It was me! So why didn't I get stuck underneath? Why did you let him get hurt instead of me?"

Christopher braced himself for the bolt of lightning that was sure to follow his impertinence. God, he'd heard, had pretty good aim. Instead, a whoop-whoop of the siren made him jump, and Christopher marveled that he'd survived.

"Hey, buddy." One of the paramedics who had been working on Dylan pulled back a corner of the blanket and faced him straight-on. "You okay in there?"

What did it look like? Christopher wiped his face with the blanket and sniffed back his tears. The paramedic had no business asking him if he was okay—not as long as Dylan lay blue and lifeless.

When Christopher didn't answer right away, the paramedic turned his attention back to the body on the stretcher. They'd already hooked needles and tubes into Dylan's arm, and maybe that would help. Still, it didn't look good. And why did the driver take so long just to get them to the little hospital in Bedford? Their red-and-blue lights lit up the darkness around them, and cars pulled off on either side of the highway.

Christopher couldn't stop thinking of all the deals he might make with God for Dylan's life, and at first he tried to come up with something that might possibly interest the Lord.

"What do you want, God?" He didn't know if he should say it out loud. Grandpa had once said a few words about "silent prayer," which seemed a little weird but okay if it worked.

You want me to go to church from now on without complaining? I'll even go to Sunday school. Twice a week like Grandma, if that makes any difference to you.

He waited for an answer, daring to peek out at Dylan's head to see if he might be sitting up and all well. Dylan never moved and still wore the oxygen mask. He could have been dead for all Christopher knew. He still looked pale and ashen, and strangely still. It occurred to Christopher that he had never seen Dylan so still before, without all the twitching and stuff. The thought scared him, and he retreated again beneath his blanket.

You want me to help Grandma more with her pies? he asked

God, trying desperately to up the ante. *I'll do triple chores as long as you want. Anything.*

He wondered how God might fill out his chore chart, the way Grandma had been doing for them the past few months. He hated the chore chart almost as much as Emily did, but this would be different.

You want me to stop arguing with Emily and Sam? Done. He found himself rocking back and forth, biting his lip until he tasted blood. *Just don't let Dylan die. Please!*

What did God want that he could give him? Christopher tried not to think of how silly or small or ridiculous he might have been, thinking about chore charts and pies as his friend lay dying. Or maybe he was already dead.

But God still remained silent when the ambulance finally rolled to a stop and the paramedics sprang into action. Christopher peeked out to see what was happening.

"Easy!" one of them called out as the back door of the ambulance swung open and they were met by a blast of cold air, a doctor, and a nurse. They yanked the rolling stretcher out with practiced movements that told Christopher they had done this once or twice before. And as they hurried away, they began comparing notes with the paramedics about respiration and heartbeat, fractures and responsiveness, and a hundred other things that might just as well have been in Greek.

And then they were gone, leaving Christopher alone for a couple of seconds to sit in an idling ambulance filled with weird medical equipment that would have been interesting at any other time. Now he just wondered what had happened to Sam, Emily, and Grandma. And was he supposed to follow the stretcher into the hospital?

He was just about to slip out the back door, too, when a nurse in a bright-flowered blouse and white pants blocked his way with a smile.

"They told me a hero named Christopher was riding along," she said, "and that I should take you inside until your grandmother gets here."

He accepted her outstretched hand as he stepped outside to a little loading area behind the hospital.

"Hero?" he asked, pulling his blankets around his shoulders.

"You pulled your little friend out from under a tractor, right?" With a gentle arm around his shoulder, she guided him through a set of automatic double doors. "You might have saved his life."

"No, you don't understand."

She couldn't know that if Dylan died, it was all his fault, and that if God really was fair, Christopher should have been met by a policeman with handcuffs rather than a smiling nurse.

But he didn't say anything else, just let her take him into a warm examination room where they took his temperature and told him his grandmother would be there in just a few minutes, and that everything would be fine.

He wasn't so sure. He still didn't know if God would go for one of his deals, or all of them.

Right now, that was the only thing that mattered.

CHARLOTTE KNEW she should have been fervently praying for Christopher's little friend Dylan, but as she sat now in the front of the fire department's aid car on the way to the little Bedford Medical Center, all she could think of was what had happened to Christopher himself.

I should have stayed with him, she thought. But in all the confusion back at the farm, somehow he'd slipped into the back of the ambulance with his friend while she made sure Sam and Emily were okay. They were going to wait back home, by the phone, until Bob or Pete showed up. While tending to them, the first ambulance had suddenly left without her.

Christopher was all alone, and even though they had called ahead to the hospital for someone to meet him, she knew she needed to be there with him at such a horrific time. She would have driven herself if they had allowed it. Now she shuddered to think of what he might be going through.

Meanwhile, the aid car driver prattled on.

"I mean, I've read about those kinds of things in the paper, you know? Some lady in Wisconsin lifted up the side of a car all by herself after it flipped on her husband. Or maybe it was in Florida. You heard about that?"

Charlotte shook her head, trying to remain polite. He was only a young man after all. He hardly seemed older than Sam.

"Anyway," he went on, "point is that sometimes you get a super adrenaline rush, kind of like the Incredible Hulk or something, and it makes you do some pretty incredible stuff."

Charlotte had no idea who the Incredible Hulk was, except that perhaps it was a cartoon character of some sort, and that her aid car driver seemed younger with each mile. Instead of keeping his eyes on the road, as she would have preferred, he glanced over at her and frowned.

"You sure you're all right?" he asked. "After all that, I mean, they're going to want to check you over once we get to the hospital, you know."

"Perhaps they will." She pointed at the road ahead of them. "In the meantime, it would be best if we don't get ourselves into yet another accident, don't you think?"

She could have bitten her tongue and hoped he might excuse her sarcasm. But every muscle in her body seemed to have been drained of its strength, and it took all her effort to remain upright.

"Wish I could have seen it though." He didn't seem to have noticed. "Just like the Incredible Hulk."

As they continued on, she let him talk, resting her eyes and moving her wet feet a little closer to where the truck's heater blew welcome hot air. As they neared town, she didn't allow the driver to turn it down, even a notch.

Yes, she supposed the story of her and the kids tipping the tractor on its side might, on the surface, sound hard to believe, but at the time it was simply the only thing they could do. The tractor had been poised at an odd angle, making their feat less than remarkable. At the same time, she was quite certain she would not have been able to even budge the machine without God's intervention, and she decided that she would explain that fact to whomever cared to know.

Oh, and the little boy's parents! How could she have forgotten? She had no idea who they were, only that their last name was Lonetree and that they were fairly new to the area. She couldn't imagine how upset they would be when they heard what had happened to their son, and especially that such a thing had happened without adult supervision. Now it would be up to Charlotte both to explain and to offer her deepest apologies.

I could have prevented this if I'd been there and more attentive, instead of immersed in my pie baking, she thought as they flashed through an intersection with the aid car lights flashing. The Bedford Medical Center would be around the next corner. With a cold shudder she finally realized how wet her clothes were and admitted to herself what she'd known all along: *This is all my fault.*

Chapter Twenty-Two

One look around the hospital waiting room reminded Charlotte why she'd come to dread this place. It brought back far too many unpleasant memories.

Yet no one working there today would remember the difficulty of Denise's birth, or how she and that precious little baby girl had both nearly died that day. But God had brought them through—brought them joy, even—and Charlotte felt certain he would again.

Wouldn't he?

Still feeling weak in the knees, she found a hard vinyl sofa and sat down. Thirty-four years ago the room had appeared much the same as it did today, with the same green institutional furniture and the same faded wall paintings of nondescript plows and covered wagons. She imagined the same dog-eared copies of *Sports Illustrated* and *Woman's Day* still decorated the waiting-room tables.

Only now it was her turn to wait here in this room, ignoring the woman with the lively toddler and the overhead television blaring a game show that no one watched.

On the TV, a smiling man waved at a stage full of dancing girls holding cards with numbers while the contestant jumped up and down in excitement. At the moment, nothing could seem more out of place. Could they not turn it off? Charlotte might have asked the young woman at the front desk but couldn't find the strength to stand. She also thought it more important right now to comfort her grandson.

Christopher, however, would not be comforted. He hung his head between his legs, the weight of the world obviously bearing down on him.

"We've all done things we wish we could have done differently, dear." She reached across and rested an arm on his shoulder. "I know you're sorry for taking the tractor out. But we'll talk to his parents together once they arrive. Your grandpa and I will be here with you, and you don't have to be afraid of anything. I'm sure it will turn out all right."

She wished she could believe her own words. Meanwhile, Christopher shook his head and looked up at her with red-rimmed eyes. He appeared as if he could burst out in tears again at any moment.

"But it's not all right, Grandma. What if I killed him?"

"No. I'm sure he's going to be all right."

She still wished she could believe her own words, even as Christopher's dread resembled her own.

"But the doctors haven't told you anything," he countered. "How do you know?"

"Well, because—" Charlotte struggled to find the right words. "Because we're praying for Dylan, that's why."

She pressed her lips together, startled at her own audacity. In a situation this grave, was it presumptuous to say such a thing? She couldn't be sure, but there—she'd said it. Dylan was going to be all right.

Fortunately or not, Christopher seemed to accept her explanation—for now—before retreating quietly once again to his own tortured thoughts. He pulled his feet up on the chair, wrapped his arms around his knees, closed his eyes, and rocked.

Oh, Christopher. She watched him in his pain, praying silently and wishing desperately that she could have taken some of that pain for him.

She had no trouble guessing who the Lonetrees were when they hurried toward the emergency entrance a few minutes later.

Mrs. Lonetree led the charge, her unkempt raven hair waving behind her and the wrinkles on her wide face pronounced in worry. She had on a pair of gray sweatpants and didn't even wear an adequate coat for the chilly November weather.

Her husband tagged along behind, wearing a bewildered expression and a sort of hollow-cheeked "Jack Sprat" look to contrast with his wife's more well-fed features. His threadbare jean jacket and grease-stained pants reminded Charlotte of a mechanic, and his rough, lined hands confirmed he was someone who spent a lot of time in manual labor. Both the man and the woman looked a bit older than Charlotte would have expected for parents of a ten- or eleven-year-old, though perhaps it was simply the world-weariness they both seemed to drag in the door with them.

"We're here for Dylan Lonetree." Dylan's mother hauled herself up to the front counter and rang the bell, though the attending nurse obviously sat right there at her station. The nurse blinked her eyes in response.

"You're the parents?" Blue light reflected off the nurse's half-glasses when she looked up from behind a computer monitor.

"I'm Brenda Lonetree," she announced in a voice loud enough to hear all the way across the room, and perhaps well beyond. She tapped her rounded fingers on the counter as she breathlessly spelled out her last name. "My husband Orrin. We came as soon as you called. Where can we see him?"

Charlotte took a deep breath and rose to her feet, unnoticed, waiting for a chance to introduce herself while the nurse motioned them through security doors. Charlotte opened her mouth too late, and then just stood there awkwardly for a moment before turning back to Christopher.

"Perhaps we'll just wait awhile longer," she told him.

She paced for the next hour or so until the Lonetrees reappeared. Charlotte heard them before she saw them.

"Yes, but we still have no answers!" insisted Mrs. Lonetree. Brenda. A flustered nurse explained that the doctors were doing all they could for Dylan and that they would simply have to wait a short while until Dr. Carr came back out. However, she added, if they would please move off to the side room and fill out a few insurance forms, they should be able to see their son again just as soon as possible.

Orrin Lonetree didn't move, just took one look at the clipboard the nurse handed him, swallowed hard, and set it back down on the counter.

"Won't do much good."

"I see." The nurse was trying her best to sound diplomatic with her hushed, measured questions. "Then, should we assume you have health coverage?"

Even from where she stood Charlotte could read the pain on their faces. With their son seriously injured they had to answer questions about the insurance they did not have.

"Oh, we got it, all right." Orrin's voice boomed just as loudly as his wife's, and his black ponytail swayed from side to side as he waved his hand for emphasis. "Problem is, it's one of them rip-off plans where you gotta pay a wicked deductible yourself. Don't know why we bothered sending in our money every month, and that's money we didn't have, when it just comes down to something like this. They got you coming and going."

"I told you we'd need it someday," his wife countered, fishing in her purse. After a minute of desperate searching she finally came up with a small card with a blue logo and faded printing. "Just in case the worst happens, like now."

"That's what I'm saying though, Brenda." Mr. Lonetree grabbed the card from her hand and studied the fine print. He handed it back to her with a grunt. "We've still got to come up with the first ten thousand. How are we going to do that?"

Now he turned to face the nurse.

"You're still going to take care of our son though, aren't you? Just 'cause we don't have the best insurance in the world . . ."

"Perhaps you could just fill out as much as you're able," interjected the nurse. "You just have a seat over there, and let me know if you have any other questions. Dr. Carr will be out shortly."

Charlotte looked down at Christopher from where she stood. By this time he seemed to be following the exchange, wide-eyed. Feeling as if they were eavesdropping on a personal conversation, she motioned for Christopher to follow as she approached them.

"Pardon me." Charlotte stopped a couple of feet away, but close enough to get a good whiff of cigarette smoke from the woman's clothing. "I'm Charlotte Stevenson, and this is my grandson Christopher. He and Dylan were—"

"*You're* Christopher?" When the woman turned her attention from the front desk to face them, Charlotte wasn't sure whether to run, stand her ground, or pull Christopher away to safety like a mama bear.

"Well, yes," Charlotte finally replied, her voice cracking. "I understand they've been spending quite a bit of time together."

By this time, Christopher's lip was quivering again, but he crossed his arms bravely and nodded. He'd already decided what he had to do. He took a deep breath before launching into his speech.

"It was all my fault, Mrs. Lonetree. I was the one who was driving the tractor when it tipped over and Dylan was hurt. My grandma didn't know anything about it. I know you'll hate me for what I've done, but I'm really, really sorry."

He gripped Charlotte's arm as he finished his speech, and tears welled up in his eyes.

Brenda bent down and rested both hands on his shoulders, looking him straight in the eyes. Poor Christopher had nowhere to hide.

"We don't hate you, Christopher." She lowered her voice a notch.

She could have slapped Christopher across the face and he would not have looked more surprised.

"You're not? Why not?"

"Well, you're Dylan's friend."

"But it wasn't my idea at first. Miss Rivkin, she was the one who told me I should help Dylan with his math. And since I already had some of the math we were studying, back in San Diego, I—"

"I know," Brenda interrupted. "In fact, I know more about you than you might guess. Every day for the past few weeks all he talks about is Christopher this, and Christopher that. He's never had a real friend like you."

"Oh." Still Christopher looked as if he couldn't believe what she was telling him, and Charlotte sighed a silent prayer of thanks for Brenda Lonetree's graciousness.

Then everyone looked up as a serious-faced doctor stepped into the room through a set of double doors. He paused in front of the group, arms folded across his green smock.

"Mr. and Mrs. Lonetree?" he asked, and the measured expression on his chiseled face revealed nothing of the nature of his news. They nodded as he went on.

"I'm Dr. Carr, and I apologize for not being able to speak with you before. We're dealing with significant injuries. Several fractures and perhaps a punctured lung. The beginning stages of hypothermia, and perhaps a bit of internal bleeding, as well. But we have several good people working on him right now, so—"

"But he's going to be all right," Mr. Lonetree interrupted. "Isn't he? He's a tough kid."

Dr. Carr held up a hand.

"The good news is that he's breathing on his own, and I have to say that's significant. My opinion is that he will come out of this with just broken bones. However, he's still under sedation, and he will be for some time, so it's a bit premature to make predictions. Let's see how he's doing in the morning. I just wanted to make sure you knew we're doing everything we can at this point, and we will keep you informed if anything changes."

He turned to go, and Charlotte could tell the Lonetrees needed to know more than they'd been told. But what could they do?

"Er, doctor?" Brenda asked. "We need to be in there with him."

The doctor paused without turning.

"I'll call you again in a few minutes, Mrs. Lonetree, after things have settled down."

She might have argued the point, but the doctor made a

hasty retreat through the double doors and was gone. They looked uncertainly at each other.

"Mrs. Lonetree," Charlotte rested a hand on the other woman's arm. "We're praying for Dylan."

Mrs. Lonetree looked at Charlotte, paused, and then enveloped her in a hug. Charlotte could feel waves of emotion from the sobbing woman, and all she could do was hold her and pat her on the back.

"I'm so sorry," Charlotte finally mumbled over and over, and she meant it more than she could say. She knew that any more words, though sincere, would sound hollow. "I should have prevented what happened. But it all happened so fast. I didn't know."

Charlotte disentangled from the embrace and sat with Brenda as they all waited for further news. Orrin paced for several minutes before leaving the room to smoke a cigarette, so he didn't notice when the double doors swung open and Bob hurried inside the waiting room. His eyes locked on Charlotte immediately, and she rushed to his arms.

"Bob!" All the emotions of the past several hours poured out as he held her in his strong grip. She wanted him to hold her like that for hours. But finally he pulled away to see that Christopher stood off to the side.

"Christopher." His voice sounded ominous but he held out his arms to enfold his grandson in a hug. "I'm glad you're all right. But you're going to tell me exactly how you came to be riding that tractor."

Christopher held on to his grandfather for a long

moment and then walked with him to a corner of the waiting room. Charlotte wasn't sure if Bob would be sharing the story of how he himself had crashed his father's tractor at age twelve. But grandfather and grandson sat closely together, and Bob rested his hands on Christopher's shoulders. Charlotte could hear Christopher's tear-filled replies to Bob's questions, even if she couldn't quite make out the words.

Don't be too hard on him, Bob, she whispered to herself.

Chapter Twenty-Three

Though Christopher wouldn't admit it, Charlotte knew how hard Friday would be for her young grandson, so she had let him stay home from school. He survived the day grim-faced and buried in chores and pie making, waiting for news of Dylan. They all did.

News came Saturday, when Charlotte set aside her spatula and hung up the telephone with a little smile. For once the breakfast dishes could wait.

"Christopher!" She called out the back door, hoping he hadn't wandered too far with the dog. Though poor Toby was improving from her earlier run-in with the raccoon, she surely wasn't improving as quickly as Christopher might have wanted. "Where are you, Christopher?"

Finally he poked his head around the corner of the barn to tell her he was just feeding the dog and changing the hay in several of the cow stalls.

"Well," she replied, "I thought you'd like to stop by the hospital with me after dropping off a few pies at Melody's. You can get back to your chores after we get back. Want to come?"

"Really? You'd let me?" He chucked a tennis ball into the field for poor Toby to chase and then bounded up to the back door himself. "I wasn't sure they were going to let us see him so soon. And Sam said you would be giving me enough chores to last me until I'm thirty-one."

Charlotte had to smile.

"We'll see about that. But I just got off the phone with Dylan's mom. He's awake this morning."

"That's good!" He didn't seem to notice when Toby hobbled up and dropped the slobbery tennis ball at his feet. "Isn't it?"

"The doctors seem to think so. Why don't you clean up while I get the latest batch of pies together, and we'll leave in ten minutes."

"Yes!" He picked up the tennis ball and heaved it once more, then turned to her. "But do you think we can stop at the bank too? I need to, uh, check on my account."

Charlotte wasn't quite certain what that meant, but the bank was on the way and it had recently started opening for a few hours on Saturday, so she didn't think that would be a problem. Ten minutes later they were headed down Heather Creek Road toward town.

"Grandma?" Christopher still wore a serious gaze as they drove past fallow fields of corn stubble, as if he was pondering something. A flock of mallards had taken refuge in a flooded area just past the Freeman farm, oblivious to the fact that Thanksgiving would be upon them in a few days. She wondered why they hadn't just headed south like most of the other birds, but her grandson's question jarred her back to the present.

"A deductible is bad, isn't it?"

She glanced over at him to make sure she'd heard him correctly.

"A deductible? Where did you hear that word?"

"You know." He shrugged. "At the hospital. Dylan's dad said they had a wicked deductible and that they would have to pay a bunch of money they didn't have."

Charlotte marveled at how much Christopher had picked up. She did her best to explain how insurance deductibles worked without getting too technical, and he nodded as she spoke.

"So the insurance company really doesn't pay, then, do they?"

"Only if it ends up costing a lot of money."

"I thought ten thousand dollars sounded like a lot of money."

"Well, yes, it does." She wondered herself what a family like the Lonetrees would do. By then they had reached Mel's Place though, and Christopher jumped into action.

"I've got it," he told her, jumping out almost before she had stopped the car. She waited behind the wheel while he trundled the half-dozen pies into the restaurant. She listened to a soothing piece of Beethoven on the public radio station while she waited and found herself closing her eyes. Christopher startled her when he hopped back into the car.

"Mrs. Melody says they need at least another two or three more dozen before Thanksgiving." He buckled his seat belt, his job complete.

"More?" She wondered if he had understood correctly.

Surely not, with less than a week until the holiday. "What kind?"

"Pumpkin, I think. I don't know. She said she would call you later today." He handed her an envelope. "And she said to give you this."

Charlotte opened the bulky envelope to discover a collection of five- and ten-dollar bills, along with a scrawled note from Melody.

"Your share from the last dozen, M."

"She said she could write you a check if you would rather have a check," added Christopher, "but just to let her know."

As a matter of fact, Charlotte would have preferred a tidier approach to accounting, but there was no sense in pushing Melody at this point. After a little mental math, she pulled out two tens and handed them over to Christopher.

"Your share," she told him, and he smiled as he examined the bills. "Isn't that right?"

"I think so. Thanks." He pointed to the road ahead. "Don't forget the bank."

"The bank. Right." She placed the car in gear, and they headed off on their next errand. And once again Christopher hopped out of the car before she'd even had a chance to turn off the ignition.

"Be right back," he told her, slamming the door behind him.

Was this the same boy who didn't know the meaning of deductibles or how his bank account worked? Something had definitely changed.

"You sure you don't want me to . . ." Her voice trailed off. Her hand on the door handle, she wondered if she should follow this time, just to be sure that he took care of his deposit correctly. But then again . . .

Maybe not, she finally decided. After all, the boy was taking the initiative, the way she'd hoped he would do. Bev Davidson at the bank would probably be there to make sure he did the right thing. He would not need his grandmother hovering over him every step of the way.

A couple minutes later, he hopped back into the car and they were on their way. Only this time, he said nothing else until they were actually walking down the hall in the hospital. Looking a little more tentative, he pulled up short by a nurses' station.

"Er, you go first," he told her, folding his arms and holding back.

"They said he was alert and talking," she replied. "I think it's okay that he see visitors. Nothing to be afraid of."

"I know. But you go ahead. I'll be there."

She nodded and led the way to Room 112, the way the nurses had directed them. Presently she came upon the open door where she recognized Brenda and Orrin Lonetree. They probably had not slept much in the past day and a half, judging by the dark circles under their eyes. Brenda, however, did smile weakly at them as they approached the door.

"I'm glad you're here," she said, stepping aside and gesturing toward the patient in the bed. "Dylan was hoping you'd come."

Dylan was propped up in bed with a frightening number

of tubes attached to his arms. Angry black and blue bruises covered his face, and a heart monitor beeped steadily nearby along with several other high-tech medical pumps, gizmos, and gadgets she could not identify. His chest and right arm were heavily wrapped, and he had already collected a couple of lovely floral bouquets and a bright silver Get Better! balloon.

"Hello, Dylan. How are you feeling?" She was almost afraid to ask. How did he look?

"Not bad," he whispered, and Charlotte figured him for either a good liar or a very fortunate boy indeed. After the way he had looked on Thursday? "Kinda sore, but not bad."

She was glad she already knew about the boy's twitching issues, so she was prepared for that part. It just looked so, well, painful. Orrin Lonetree beamed.

"I told the doctor he was a tough little guy." He patted Dylan on the head. "They wouldn't believe me at first. How many kids do you know can have a tractor fall on top of them and come out two days later looking like this?"

Christopher hung back, looking shy and uncertain. Dylan noticed his visitor and tried to raise his hand in greeting.

"I get to drive the tractor next time instead of you," he told Christopher in a quiet voice, a hint of a smile playing his chapped lips. "Okay?"

"I can guarantee you there's not going to be any tractor riding for a while," said Charlotte, and she was grateful for the nervous laughs of support from Dylan's parents. It could have been much worse, though their poor son still looked very much in pain. A duty nurse must have heard the noise and poked her head in from the hall.

"Sorry to break up the party," she told them, "but Dr. Carr wants to take a look at how our star patient is doing."

Charlotte could take the hint, and she immediately stepped toward the door.

"We should go."

She said her good-byes but noticed Christopher hung back at the side of the bed.

"Christopher?" She called to him from the hallway.

"Be right there."

Apparently he leaned close to say something else to his friend, and Dylan responded with his usual jerking movements—and a faint smile.

"I'm not mad," replied Dylan, his voice soft and low.

"But—" Christopher tried to explain, but Dylan would have none of it.

"I told you, it's not your fault, okay?" Dylan told him. "I don't blame you. Nobody blames you. It was just an accident."

Charlotte knew Christopher's grandfather might have something else to say about the matter, but she let it go for now. There would be plenty of time to talk about the consequences of his misbehavior.

Meanwhile Christopher pulled out an envelope from his pocket and laid it next to Dylan on his bed, saying something she could not make out. She smiled and wondered when he'd had time to buy a get-well card.

BY THE TIME THEY HAD STOPPED at the grocery store for more nutmeg and made it home to Heather Creek

Farm, a light November snow had begun to fall, dusting fields with white but leaving the driveway clear.

"You're popular today, Mom." Pete greeted them in the driveway and held the car door open. "Phone's been ringing off the hook for you. Maybe you should get a cell phone."

"What do you mean?" Charlotte handed him the paper sack with her groceries and followed him into the kitchen.

"Well, first Melody called a couple of times to say something about how donations are already coming in. Do you know what she's talking about?"

"Donations?" Charlotte scratched her head and looked to Christopher for a clue, but he had already disappeared. "I'm afraid I haven't any idea, but I suppose I'll find out."

"Well, she wasn't making much sense," added Pete, twirling his green and gold AA Tractor Supply cap in his hand, "but I can tell you she was pretty pumped up about it."

"*Hmm*. Pumped. Was that all?"

"Actually, no. Somebody named Brenda Lonetree called just a few minutes ago, and I couldn't tell if she was hopping mad at you or if she was crying, or what."

"Brenda Lonetree?" Charlotte's heart leaped to her throat as she wondered why Dylan's mother would be calling.

"That's what she said. She was just really emotional, kind of off the deep end. Is that the mom of—"

She nodded an answer to his unfinished question.

"Right," he went on. "Anyway, she wanted you to call her back right away. She said, 'the minute she steps in the door'—"

"Did you get her number?" Charlotte grabbed the note from Pete's hand and hurried for the kitchen phone. By the time she had Brenda Lonetree on the line, she had gathered a bit of an audience. Pete stood off to the side, pretending not to listen in while Sam and Emily peeked down from the stairway with wide eyes.

"My son said you called, Brenda." She imagined Mrs. Lonetree on the other end of the line, distraught at whatever had just happened. Yes, Dylan had looked much improved when they were there this morning, but anything could have happened in the meantime. "Is there something wrong?"

Brenda Lonetree sounded breathless on the other end.

"No—yes . . . I mean, I really don't know what to say about this."

"It's all right." Now Charlotte was more than puzzled. Had something happened, or not? "You can tell me. Was it something Dr. Carr told you?"

"No, no. He didn't tell us anything we didn't already know. It's your grandson." She hesitated before going on. "He left an envelope with Dylan when you were here. He told Dylan to give it to Orrin and me."

"Well, I'm so glad to hear that there's no bad news about Dylan." Charlotte breathed a sigh of relief. "But was it a, a card of some kind?"

"No, that's just it. It was cash. And a lot of it, for a little boy."

Charlotte heard a man's voice in the background, obviously filling Brenda in on the details.

"Right. Sixty-two dollars and fifty-three cents."

The pieces fell into place: Christopher listening intently. Christopher asking about deductibles. Christopher going into the bank, coming out with an envelope. So he'd made a withdrawal and not a deposit! He'd been planning it all along. She covered the phone's mouthpiece and whispered to Pete.

"Go get Christopher and bring him here, please. Right away!"

Pete nodded gravely and slipped out the door while Sam and Emily gave up their lurking and came down the stairs to hear what was really going on.

"Mrs. Stevenson?" Brenda Lonetree interrupted her thoughts. "Are you still there?"

"Yes. Yes, of course." Charlotte shook her head and chose her words carefully. "We're looking for Christopher right now, so we'll be able to talk to him. Of course I can't speak for him, but I can tell you he was very concerned about Dylan. I'm sure you knew he feels terribly responsible for what happened. Perhaps this is his way of helping out."

"Well, sure. And I've got to say we're very touched. But we can't let him empty his piggybank like this, y'know? We just can't accept it."

Charlotte paused when Christopher appeared at the back door, looking mortified. Her heart melted at the sight.

"Brenda, I'd like to speak with Christopher. Perhaps it would help if we knew just what he's thinking, rather than just assuming. May I call you again as soon as I find out more?"

As Charlotte hung up the phone, Christopher remained standing in the doorway looking down, his feet rooted. Fortunately, Pete came up behind him and scooted him inside, or he might never have moved.

"Am I in more trouble?" he whispered.

At a time like this she would have gathered him up in her arms, if he had only let her. Instead she sat down at a kitchen chair and motioned for him to join her. He shuffled a little closer, obviously still not sure of his status. Sam and Emily followed the conversation. She tried not to sound like a prosecuting attorney.

"You're not in any more trouble than you already were, dear. I just have to know something: Did you withdraw all the money from your account and give it to the Lonetrees?"

"Uh . . ." He paused for a moment, as if trying to decide if what he said would incriminate him. "Not all of it."

He stood next to the kitchen table but dug at an imaginary hole in the linoleum.

"Then how much did you leave in, Christopher?"

"Twenty-five."

"Oh." That didn't seem to add up with the figure Brenda Lonetree had just given her. Had he really saved so much in such a short time? "So you left twenty-five dollars in . . . ?"

He paused again before adding a soft postscript.

"Not twenty-five *dollars*, Grandma."

"You mean twenty-five . . . *cents*?"

"You told me I always had to leave something in there. So I did. I was just trying to do the right thing after messing up so bad the other day."

Charlotte studied his face but could see nothing but frightened sincerity. She knew Christopher wasn't trying to fool anyone. But now Sam joined the interrogation from where he leaned against the refrigerator.

"You gave all your pie money away?" he said, his jaw practically hanging open in amazement. "What about the Nintendo? What about the weather station you were going to buy?"

Emily looked nearly as stunned at the news but said nothing.

"They need it," replied Christopher, sounding meeker than ever. "It's going to cost them big bucks to have Dylan stay in the hospital, and they have a wicked deductible."

"A deductible?" Sam looked confused.

"It means they have to pay the insurance company, plus they have to pay the hospital too. It's like paying double," Christopher explained.

That effectively quieted Christopher's older brother, though Charlotte could tell from his incredulous expression that he still didn't fully understand what Christopher was doing, or why.

And then something else dawned on her.

"Wait a minute," she said. "Did you mention anything to Melody about the Lonetrees when we stopped by the restaurant this morning?"

"No!" This time he was adamant, and his eyebrows wrinkled down to emphasize his innocence. "I know better'n that. I didn't say nothing about Dylan, not to nobody."

She resisted the temptation to correct his grammar. But though she had her suspicions, now she had to find out exactly what Melody was up to.

Chapter Twenty-Four

"I'm sorry, Charlotte." Melody's voice came over the phone so loud and clear that almost anyone in the Stevensons' kitchen could hear just as well as she. "I should have told you yesterday morning when Christopher dropped by with the pies. But it was just a spontaneous thing. You know how that is."

"Well, not really I don't, but . . ." Charlotte stirred her spaghetti sauce as she talked. Bob and Pete had already drifted into the kitchen for Sunday supper, following their noses and washing their dirty hands in the sink the way she'd told them not to at least a thousand times. Melody's voice escaped from the telephone handset, loud and clear.

"But surely you can't have a problem with us collecting money for the Lonetrees," she said. "Do you?"

"No, certainly not. It seems like a very nice thing to do. I just don't know how you found out about it so quickly. Are you sure Christopher didn't tell you?"

"Oh, you mean when he came in the restaurant yesterday morning?" She laughed. "No, your Christopher didn't say anything. You could ask him yourself. He just walked right in with that big box of yours and left the pies on the counter, just the way he was supposed to. Very businesslike. You must have him trained. In fact, I was sort of wondering why he looked so serious. He didn't say much of anything the way he usually does."

"Well, then what gave you the idea that there even *was* a need?"

"Actually, it was a nurse down at the hospital when I called Thursday night, just to be sure you were all okay."

"The admitting nurse?" Charlotte groaned, expecting the worst.

"No, it's not what you think." Melody scrambled to fill in the details. "Let me just explain. You know that Rick Barnes always carries a police scanner on his belt, and he was in the restaurant late Thursday afternoon, getting a cup of coffee, when all the commotion started happening. I haven't seen him move that fast in a long time."

Charlotte couldn't help chuckling at the thought of their portly local newspaper editor rushing out of Mel's Place with his radio in hand in pursuit of a hot story. Her smile froze when she realized he hadn't yet contacted her, but that he probably would—sooner rather than later. "So you knew as soon as it happened." Charlotte repeated what they now both knew. "But the nurse didn't tell you about their finances, did she? That wouldn't be right. She could be fired for something like that."

"Oh no, no. I told you nobody is breaking patient confidentiality. I just said something like I thought it was dreadful what had happened to the poor little boy, and I wondered if they had any insurance."

"And what did she say?"

"So then I asked her, I said, 'Well, do you think they would appreciate it if we took a collection for their medical expenses? They're going to have a lot after this accident, aren't they?' That's pretty much exactly the words I used."

"And she said—"

"And she said yes, it wasn't any secret that the boy's hospital stay would be expensive. Anybody could guess as much. And then she just told me that if she were in Brenda Lonetree's shoes, she was sure without a doubt that she would appreciate a collection. Without a doubt. Those are the words she used. Without a doubt."

"Mel—"

Melody wasn't listening.

"Too bad Cindi Slate on the TV couldn't hear about this story. Fifty cents from every slice of pie sold at Mel's Place, donated to the Dylan Lonetree fund. Don't you think that sounds like a story the television networks would want to carry?"

"Good publicity for you."

"Charlotte Stevenson! I just think it could be as big as the pie story. Do you know how many orders we're still getting from that? People are still calling, and they've told their friends, who have told their friends. Somebody said a food magazine in Omaha picked up the story. Are you sure you can keep up with all the orders?"

"Melody—" Charlotte ignored the question and tried warning her friend. "Don't you think we've already had our fifteen minutes of fame?"

"Nothing wrong with having twenty now, is there? Especially if it's for a good cause."

Now Charlotte was getting the picture, though she still had no idea how to explain it to the Lonetrees. She just shook her head in amazement.

"I still can't believe how quickly everyone finds out about a situation like this."

"Small town. We get the word out, even better than network television. So you're going to explain everything to Brenda Lonetree?"

Charlotte sighed, wondering how she had drawn this assignment. Perhaps it didn't need to be as awkward as she feared.

"I'll tell her."

BY THE TIME CHARLOTTE CAUGHT UP with Brenda and her family the next day she had to explain not only Christopher's $62.53 and the fifty cents a pie slice fund, but apparently also how a jar on the counter at Melody's had already started to fill up with change and dollar bills.

What's more, the women's ministry leaders at Bedford Community Church had just set a date for a special Pancake Feed benefit, with all proceeds going to help offset the family's medical expenses. Word was getting around as quickly as it normally did in Bedford. Charlotte stood with Dylan's mom in the hospital hallway, trying to explain all the details.

"I know it's not much," she told Brenda, trying her best to sound casual, "especially not compared to the bills you must be facing. But everyone I've talked to expressed the hope that in the months to come we can, you know, perhaps help with the rest, as well."

Brenda Lonetree gripped Charlotte's hands while tears flowed unchecked.

"You don't even know us," she began, and her voice wavered as if she might break down, while her grip threatened to cut off the circulation. "We don't even go to your church."

"That's not the point."

"We attend mass at Holy Family once in a while."

Charlotte squeezed back."Nobody asked where you went to church," she replied. "People just want to show you that they care. I hope that's all right with your family."

"I appreciate it more than you can imagine."

Finally Brenda released her grip and wiped her tears. Charlotte fished for a tissue in her purse but found none, while the other woman glanced nervously down the hall at the sound of hurried footsteps. "But there's something you should understand about my husband. You see, Orrin—"

Her voice faded as her husband approached, a storm on his face when he noticed Charlotte. He couldn't be upset about the gradually improving condition of his son, could he?

"Orrin," Brenda stood in her husband's way, but he walked quickly around them to enter Dylan's room. He completely avoided looking at Charlotte and then stopped dead in the doorway with his back to both of them.

"Look," he said, bracing himself against the doorjamb. Charlotte had a sinking feeling this was what Brenda had started to warn her about. "I don't know where everybody got the idea that we were the charity case of the year."

Charlotte winced at his words, preparing for what would come next.

"Orrin," began his wife, "they're just trying to—"

"I know what they're just trying to do, Brenda." He cut her off with a raised hand, and Charlotte could see him square his shoulders before he turned around. Suddenly, she wished she had never come to the hospital this time. Now he faced them but kept his eyes focused on the well-polished gray tile floor.

"We appreciate what you're doing, Mrs. Stevenson, especially since it was your kid's fault what happened."

Charlotte gasped as he went on.

"And I don't fault him none for trying to make it right, as much as he knows how. He's a good kid. We've already told you he's been a good friend to our Dylan. But maybe you can tell your pal at the restaurant that we can take care of ourselves."

He didn't wait for a reply, even if Charlotte could have managed to say something. Instead he swiveled on his heel, stepped into his son's room, and shut the door behind him. Charlotte stepped away, nearly knocking over a linen cart just behind her.

"I should go."

"No, wait." Brenda took Charlotte's hand again, a pleading look on her face. "I'm sorry for my husband. He was really touched by what your son did with the money and all, but when he saw what was going on at Melody's, I'm afraid he just got sort of, you know, embarrassed by the whole thing."

"I understand." Charlotte nodded, and it occurred to her that her own husband might have reacted in a similar way.

Something about men and their pride.

"I'll . . ." Brenda headed for the door herself. "I'll talk to him about it again. Maybe he'll change his mind. Give him some time."

Charlotte nodded, not knowing what else to do.

"And I'll speak to Melody about it as well," Charlotte answered. "I, we really should have checked with you first before going overboard with all the collections. It just all seemed to happen so quickly. I'm very sorry."

"No, no. There's no reason to be sorry."

"Brenda!" Orrin Lonetree's voice came through the closed door, and the strident tone couldn't be mistaken. Brenda moved nervously to the door, and Charlotte felt her heart go out to the younger woman. Surely there was something else they could do for her, for the family, without wounding Orrin Lonetree's fragile pride.

"I'm sorry this has caused you so much trouble," Charlotte told her in parting. "You know that wasn't the intent."

Brenda nodded and slipped behind the door, looking more helpless and alone than she had before. Unfortunately, Charlotte had a feeling the trouble wasn't over yet—a foreboding that was confirmed when she noticed Rick Barnes headed her direction. His red face and puffing cheeks betrayed the fact that he spent most of his time behind a computer monitor, writing and editing stories for the weekly *Bedford Leader*. A digital camera swung from side to side from a strap around his neck.

"There you are, Miz Stevenson." He held up a finger to get her attention, though it was hardly necessary. "I was hoping you'd tell me a little about the accident out on your place the other day. Maybe about the fund for the Lonetree family, if you know anything about that. Have a moment?"

She sighed and checked her watch. In truth she really should be back home by now, starting another batch of pies. But he'd cornered her, and she couldn't be rude.

"I'm honestly not sure how much I can help you, Mr. Barnes. But perhaps if you have specific questions, I can tell you what I know while we're walking out to my car."

Chapter Twenty-Five

"Oooh, it's Emily Slater, famous pie-maker!" A gaggle of girls headed by Nicole Evans caught up to Emily on her way to the cafeteria just before noon on Wednesday.

Not again.

Emily drew herself up, gripped her science text to her chest, and pretended not to notice when Nicole bumped up beside her. What was that girl's problem?

"So will you sign my newspaper?" asked Nicole. "I've never known anyone who was famous before."

Nicole's friends all snickered on cue while Nicole held out a newspaper and a Sharpie pen as if she was dead serious.

Maybe I'd better play along, thought Emily, taking the other girl's copy of the *Bedford Leader*. It was folded back to the front-page article on how the community was getting behind the Lonetree family, and how sales of local pies had helped the effort. Emily's name was mentioned in the last paragraph, along with Sam's and Christopher's.

"Really," added Nicole in a sugar-sweet voice. "I think it's *sooo* cool."

Emily scribbled her signature in the margin of the article, near the bottom, and handed it back. With barely disguised sarcasm Nicole passed it around for the others to see, but it was clear she wasn't done.

"I was wondering, you don't actually eat those pies, do you? I mean, don't pies have lard in them? And since lard is pig fat, well, you wouldn't touch that, I'm sure. That wouldn't be veggy-tarian."

"Grandma doesn't use lard in her recipes."

"You're sure?" Nicole acted disappointed as she crumpled and tossed the signed newspaper into a nearby trash can. "Crisco then?"

Emily thought Crisco was vegetable oil but still wasn't quite sure where this was going, except to give her a hard time. By now they had arrived at the cafeteria though, and everyone seemed to pause at the door, sniffing the air.

"What is that *awful* stink?" asked Nicole. No one had ever accused her of having delicate manners.

But as they moved forward in line, they soon discovered the source of the aroma—which Emily would have described as nutty or mushroomy, with a hint of sweetness. Something was different, all right. And when the others saw a large whiteboard sign set up on an easel next to the line by the door, they all groaned.

"No turkey for early Thanksgiving?" asked Nicole, parking her hands on her hips. "What is this?"

"We've never not had turkey and stuffing for Thanksgiving," someone else announced. This time the lunch line supervisor overheard their complaining.

"You're going to like this, kids," said Nancy Evans, the

pastor's wife and Nicole's mother. She gave Emily a wink. "It wasn't on the published menu, but I think we were all due for a change. Don't you, Nicole?"

"Uh—" Nicole looked ready to escape the cafeteria without eating, and her mouth had turned down in disgust. "I still can't believe it. I would never even *think* of eating something like this."

Nicole's last words made Emily freeze in recognition, as if she had just heard her own words played back to her. From this side of the conversation, it didn't sound too pretty.

Did I really sound that whiney? she wondered. But no, she remembered. She had sounded worse, and more obnoxious, and louder. Loud enough for Mrs. Evans to hear.

And realizing how she'd sounded gave her a queasy feeling in the pit of her stomach. It had nothing to do with how good the food smelled, or how cool the menu sounded.

So Emily just listened as kids around her read the menu.

"Choice of kidney bean and sweet potato chili," began a boy in front of her. "Sweet potato, huh? No meat?"

That's right; no meat. Wasn't that the idea? He didn't seem to quite appreciate that particular feature of vegetarian dishes, and she didn't care to explain it to him.

"Butternut squash with rice and onion stuffing," continued another. "Creamed corn, cranberry chutney—what the heck is chutney?"

Emily didn't want to explain, but Mrs. Evans did a pretty good job of it from behind the serving line.

"You just taste it and see, Justin." She ladled the doubtful kid a generous dollop of the corn pudding too. "It's like a sweet fruit salsa, with lots of good spices. You're going to like it."

"Guaranteed?" He still wasn't so sure as he gave his tray another sniff. But at least he took it back to his seat, which was a step in the right direction.

Other kids coming up in line didn't miss the little note in small letters at the bottom though.

Thanks go to Emily Slater for all the great suggestions! Enjoy!

Emily wasn't sure whether to smile or duck for cover as she made her way to the head of the line. A couple of kids actually clapped and cheered, though she couldn't be sure if they were serious or just teasing her like Nicole, or even if the clapping would be followed by people attacking her with their chutney. Maybe she deserved it, the way she had once treated Mrs. Evans. Still, she held out her tray as the cafeteria lady ladled a generous helping of squash on her plate.

"Principal Duncan said to tell you he and the school board appreciated your suggestions," said Mrs. Evans. "We might even try a more healthy vegetarian menu like this on some other days. I had no idea it was going to turn out so well."

"It does smell good," replied Emily, still unsure what to say. "And thanks for, well, maybe you can tell Mr. Duncan thanks for me?"

"Oh, I suppose I could." Mrs. Evans smiled. "But it would probably be easier if you did it yourself."

The principal had just sidled up in back of Emily to check out the special Thanksgiving feast himself.

"These ladies really outdid themselves this time, didn't

they, Emily?" The principal smiled at them like a politician looking for votes, but Emily had to agree.

Behind them, another boy groaned all over again when he saw the menu.

"Can't I just have a corn dog with fries?" he asked.

Mr. Duncan pointed his way with a stern look.

"Not on your life, Shawn. We're going to teach you to appreciate healthy food if it kills you!"

The rest of the students laughed at the joke. "By the way, Emily," Mr. Duncan snapped her back to reality, "that was a real nice article in the *Leader* about the Lonetrees, don't you think?"

Emily wasn't sure how to answer but nodded her agreement as the principal went on. She did her best not to look at Nicole.

"I had no idea you were helping your grandmother all this time with the pies, and how it's helping that family."

Emily stood in the middle of the cafeteria, holding her tray as the crowds flowed around her, and she felt like a fraud.

Sure, she had helped Grandma in the kitchen. But so had Christopher. And now Christopher had given his life savings to help the Lonetrees.

She shook her head but could not lose the idea that now haunted her. And when her friend Ashley stepped into the cafeteria she hurried over to hold out her tray.

"Here," she told Ashley, handing over the food. "Take this. I haven't touched anything."

"What?" Ashley obviously didn't get it. "Aren't you hungry? This is Emily Slater Menu Day. This is your day, girl!"

Without an answer, Emily hurried out of the cafeteria before anyone else noticed her, or asked her for a stupid autograph, or told her she had done anything special. She ran her fingers through her hair as she escaped down the hallway, afraid of what she was thinking.

She did know where to find Sam though, and caught his eye from a distance. He would be hanging out with some of his friends just outside the gym, drinking sodas and being generally loud and obnoxious. She knew better than to walk right up to them, but motioned him over with a subtle jerk of her chin. He looked away but excused himself a few seconds later, walking to where she stood behind the Coke machine.

"Hey, sis," he greeted her. "I thought you'd be in the cafeteria, chowing down on veggie delight."

"So you heard about that?"

"Are you kidding? I had to eat three hot dogs in front of the guys today just to prove I ate meat and wasn't weird like you."

"Taste good?"

He shrugged. "Made me gag. Now, what do you need?"

He looked around again, probably just to be sure no one saw him hanging around with his little sister. At this point though, she didn't care much.

She just wasn't sure how to tell him what she'd been thinking.

Chapter Twenty-Six

When the phone rang Wednesday afternoon Charlotte realized she'd been dozing at her own kitchen sink, still holding a half-washed dish from a distant breakfast. "I'll get it, Grandma!" Emily yelled.

She did, but a moment later surrendered the receiver to Charlotte with a whispered, "Melody."

No surprise there. Every other phone call for the past two weeks had been Melody. The good news was that this close to Thanksgiving, another order would be unlikely. But Melody sounded unsure.

"Promise me you won't hate me for this, Char."

Charlotte breathed in sharply and shifted the phone to her other ear. This could not be good.

"Of course not, Melody. Just don't tell me you have another order." She paused when Melody didn't answer right away. "Oh, Melody. Do you?"

"Well, here's the thing. A gal called me this morning early all the way from Grand Island, and apparently she's been planning a big family reunion for Thanksgiving, so people are flying in from all parts of the country, but her elderly mother isn't expected to live more than a couple months."

"I'm sorry to hear that, but—"

"Right, and now she just heard about our special recipe apple-caramel pie. It was something her mother had loved as a child, and they thought it would just be a wonderful gesture if—"

"How many, Melody?" Charlotte was glad Melody couldn't see the frown that had slipped across her face.

"Well, it's a very large family from what I'm told, and she said they would come pick them up in person, so we don't have to deliver them."

"How many?"

"Just three."

Charlotte sighed with relief. "That's all?"

"And three pumpkin. But just tell me no, Charlotte, and I'll call her back. I know it's the day before Thanksgiving, and you have your own family to think about, your own meals to cook. Believe me—"

"I'll do it." She glanced over at the refrigerator where her turkey had been thawing, a nice fifteen-pounder, and wondered when she would ever have time to prepare their own Thanksgiving meal.

"Are you sure? They wanted a cherry-berry, too, if you could possibly manage that?"

"And?"

"And nothing. That's it. I'll even come to your place and pick them up, so you don't have to drive them into town. How about that? What should I tell her?"

Three apple-caramel, three pumpkin, and a cherry-berry. Charlotte mentally tallied her remaining supplies, just to be sure she could cover the order. Finally she sighed and her shoulders sagged.

"I said I'll do it. I mean, *we'll* do it, if I can round up the kids."

By this time Melody wasn't arguing, and her voice lifted noticeably.

"You're an angel of mercy, Charlotte Stevenson. So I told her she could stop by the restaurant tomorrow and pick it up herself, if the roads weren't too icy or sloppy, that is, so . . ."

"It sounds as if you had everything covered. But Mel? This will be the last order, won't it?"

By that time Emily had begun to slip out of the kitchen, but Charlotte caught her eye and gestured her granddaughter back. No way was Charlotte doing this alone. She said her good-byes, hung up the phone, and found Christopher on the living room floor, drawing pictures of his latest space station creation. He looked up at her with an amused expression on his face.

"It's okay, Grandma." At least Christopher seemed to understand, bless his heart. "But I was just wondering. Are we just going to be making Thanksgiving for other families this year?"

And this boy was what, just ten years old?

"Don't you worry." Charlotte hesitated. "We'll have a wonderful meal together tomorrow."

"Really?" Unfortunately, he'd learned enough about

cooking in the past month to know better. "Who's going to cook it? And when?"

Charlotte didn't have a good answer for him then, and didn't have a good answer for him later as they went through the routine of laying out ingredients, pulling out flour and pie tins, and arranging mixing bowls for each variety of pie. One would hardly guess that these kids hadn't known a measuring cup from a rolling pin only a few short weeks ago.

But had she achieved her goal of bringing them closer together, of teaching them her value of hard work? Charlotte honestly couldn't be sure. All she knew was that the more they worked in her mother-in-law's trim kitchen, the more she just wanted to be done with the whole affair.

Problem was, she'd been chained to the double oven so much in the past few weeks, she had barely found time to plan the usual Thanksgiving meal. She wasn't even sure she had a plan.

Pete came tromping up the stairs later that evening, interrupting her bone-weary thoughts and shaking the sleet off his coat.

"Whew!" he exclaimed, stopping at the top of the stairs. "Pretty messy out there."

No one answered. They could all watch the nasty weather out the window while tiny ice pellets hit the glass with a nice sort of musical chaos. Emily kept rolling, Christopher kept mixing, and Charlotte checked the oven.

"Hmm." He tried again. "Thought I was going to smell

something good when I got up here, like stuffing. Is that all coming tomorrow?"

Still no one answered until Christopher stopped his mixing and looked straight at his uncle.

"We're not going to have turkey this year, Uncle Pete."

"Oh." Uncle Pete looked good and surprised. "Ham, then?"

"Not ham, either."

Charlotte wondered if her little grandson had been rooting around in the freezer, or what. How did he know what she had, or not?

"What Christopher means," she explained as she slid a ready pie onto a well-heated rack, "is that I just haven't started on tomorrow's dinner yet. Everything's just been so busy, you know, with all this pie mania."

He nodded as the door opened once again and heavy footsteps told Charlotte that Bob was advancing up the stairs.

"Hey, Pete," he began, "have you seen your—"

He stopped when he reached the top.

"—mother?"

Pete grabbed a pile of keys from a coffee table and made his exit. "Just so you know," he told his dad, "those things they're working on are not turkeys, and they're not for us."

Bob stood rubbing the stubble on his chin, and Charlotte knew the inevitable comment was coming.

"I thought you said you were done," he said, his arms crossed. She thought his expression softened a bit when she explained about Melody's emergency phone call, but not much.

"Well," he finally conceded, "as long as there's no more after this."

"Amen to that," whispered Emily, almost under her breath.

"Look, everybody." Charlotte straightened her apron and looked at everyone. "I'm really sorry this didn't turn out quite the way I—the way we—hoped it would. Things got a little out of hand."

"You think?" Emily stopped rolling out dough long enough to add her opinion as Charlotte continued, and the sarcasm stung.

"But I still believe we've learned a few things, don't you all?" No one answered right away, and she felt unwelcome tears of exhaustion ready to spill over. That wasn't the answer she was looking for just then. "Well, I'm telling Melody she's going to have to find another pie maker after Thanksgiving. But at least we didn't quit. Right?"

When no one answered something finally snapped Charlotte's frayed nerves, and still they all just looked at her as if she'd been speaking Chinese. Even Bob, who should have known better. A little puzzlement from the kids she could handle, but not from Bob.

Please! How about a little support?

"Uh, we need to get back to work," Bob said, and that was the end of it for Charlotte for now. Pie deadline or not, she had to take a break—even just for an hour or two.

So without another word she yanked off her apron and

tossed it aside, running down the stairs and pushing outside, nearly knocking down Sam in the process.

"Grandma?" he backed away and almost dropped the pie box in his arms.

"And that goes for you too!" she told him, feeling silly and indignant and exhausted all at the same time. Mostly exhausted.

"What?" He wrinkled his eyebrows in confusion. "I have to tell you something. I—"

"Please, Sam." She held up her hand. "Just a little later."

All she wanted was to lock the door behind her, lose herself under the covers of her bed for an hour or two, and perhaps have a good long cry into her down pillow. She deserved it.

She looked up at the sky as she hurried toward the house and blinked at the ice pellets. Despite the pain, they felt almost refreshing as she walked around outside to clear her head.

They can do without me for just a few minutes.

A little hibernation right now sounded pretty good. Maybe if she just found a place to close her eyes for ten minutes . . .

THE NEXT THING CHARLOTTE KNEW, a soft knock at her bedroom door helped bring her back to the present—whenever that might have been. She sat up in bed and wondered at the gray light filtering in through her lace bedroom curtains.

She glanced at the red numbers of her bedside clock

once more and gasped. She hadn't been napping for just a little while.

"Oh no." She jumped up, panic seizing her at the sight of daylight. She'd honestly only meant to rest her eyes for a moment, but now somehow she'd managed to sleep through the night and well into the next morning. How in the world?

"Grandma!" Christopher's voice came through the bedroom door. "Open up! We're all going to deliver the last pies, and you're coming along."

"But—" Despite her better judgment she stumbled to the door and twisted the doorknob lock open. Her eyes felt puffy beyond hope. "But we're not done with them yet."

"They're done." Bob stood in the doorway, framed by the hallway light. "You should have seen these kids. All three of them. They're experts."

"All three?" She shook the cobwebs from her brain, trying to understand what they were telling her. Bob, Christopher, Emily, and Sam crowded in behind. "By yourselves?"

"The pies are ready," Pete announced from downstairs, "and your last customers are waiting. So let's put a coat on, Mom, and get this show on the road."

Charlotte still wasn't sure exactly what was going on, but she dressed quickly, and brushed her teeth and brushed her hair. The kids were already waiting in her idling car, with Emily and Christopher balancing a towel-wrapped pie between them in the backseat and Sam waiting behind the wheel.

"No other deliveries today, Sam?" she asked, and he shook his head.

"That's what I was trying to tell you last night, Grandma. I asked Brad for a couple days off, so I could help more with the pies."

"You did?" The news made Charlotte feel even smaller for the way she had snapped at him the night before. "I'm—"

"Let's go!" Bob yelled. "You look fine."

She didn't believe a word of it but slipped into the passenger seat of her car and closed the door as the men piled into Pete's truck and it roared to life. Inside the car, though, she was met by the familiar comforting aroma of cherry-berry pie—as well as something else. *Hmm.*

One of them smells a little different, she thought. *I wonder if the kids strayed from my recipe.*

Besides that, how could they have finished the crusts without her help? Would they have browned everything just right without letting them burn? What about all the other pies? And what about her own Thanksgiving meal, still unprepared?

"Wait a minute!" Her head finally cleared as she remembered what day it was and what was wrong with this scene. "Melody promised me she would pick the pies up herself. She's probably on her way here now."

"It's okay, Grandma." Emily sounded sure of herself.

"And my turkey!" Charlotte reached for the door handle to climb back out. "You don't understand. I need to put it into the oven!"

Sam just put the car into gear, shook his head, and grinned as they started down the driveway.

"Everything's under control, Grandma. Trust me."

Chapter Twenty-Seven

Charlotte tried to trust them, but she knew something strange was going on when Sam turned left onto Oldham Street behind Pete before they reached downtown. The car slid only a little on the icy roadway as Emily warned him to slow down.

"You got a backseat driver's license?" asked Sam, not one to be coached by his little sister.

"Don't need one when you're going to kill us all," she quipped. "You just need to slow—"

"Cut it out, you guys!" Christopher stepped into the argument. "Why don't you both just stop arguing?"

"*Hmm.*" Sam frowned and continued on. "She started it."

"This isn't the way to Mel's Place, Sam." Charlotte gripped the armrest and told him what he must have already known.

"It's okay, Grandma," he assured her, and a small grin played on his face. "We know where we're going."

Pete promptly fishtailed his way into the driveway of a modest two-story home, and Sam followed. She gave Sam a questioning look.

"Just a quick delivery," he told her, "but you have to come along."

"Not the way I look," she told him, but they had already opened the doors and quickly eased her out of her seat. A minute later they all paraded up the walkway and piled onto a sagging front porch. A small, hand-lettered sign hanging by the front door finally told her that they were knocking on the Lonetrees' door.

"He got home from the hospital." Christopher took the lead with a pie in hand.

"You made them an extra pie?" asked Charlotte. "What if they don't know we're coming?"

"Not to worry, Mom." This time it was Pete's turn to reassure her as they waited. "These kids have everything under control."

Well, she was glad someone did. For her part, Charlotte still wondered what these young people were doing. But judging by the way Sam and Emily whispered to each other, they obviously had something more in mind than just delivering a friendly Thanksgiving pie.

A moment later Brenda Lonetree greeted them at the door and welcomed them in with a smile.

"It's so nice of you to come," she told them, taking Charlotte's hand. Charlotte returned the smile and hoped she didn't look as bewildered as she felt.

The inside of the Lonetree home was spare but clean, with mismatched furniture and a worn, harvest gold sofa that looked as if it might have come from a Goodwill store. Family pictures of dark-eyed relatives lined the wall of the short hallway leading past a small kitchen.

"I hope we're not—" Charlotte began to apologize and then changed her mind as they all crowded into Dylan's little room, where he'd been propped up in his bed directly beneath one of several airplane posters. His face looked scrubbed, his cheeks red, and his jet black hair was neatly slicked back.

His parents stood off to the side. Brenda Lonetree held on to her forced smile of welcome while her husband crossed his arms.

"Happy Thanksgiving!" Christopher held up his prize. "It's cherry-berry, and we made it ourselves. I mean, even without Grandma's help, but it's our great-grandma's recipe.

"We've heard about that recipe of yours." Dylan's mom accepted the gift while his dad leaned closer for a good whiff. His eyes widened a little despite himself.

Well, perhaps the kids knew what they were doing after all. A bit of pie diplomacy seemed to go a long way toward melting Orrin Lonetree's steely countenance.

"Just like Mom's," said Pete, looking at his father. "Don't you think?"

"Uh—" Bob looked over at Charlotte. "Will I get in trouble if I say yes?"

"No, I'm sure he's right." She turned to Emily to add her compliments. "I'm sure it's as good as . . . my mother-in-law used to make. Her favorite was the cherry-berry as well. Although I don't know how she ate so much of it and still stayed as tiny as a bird."

Across the small room Emily elbowed Sam.

"Okay, okay," he mumbled, and drew himself up. He felt the pocket of his red ski jacket and cleared his throat.

"Uh, I have something to say," he announced to the group. Charlotte looked to Bob for a clue, but he only shook his head and directed her back with a glance toward Sam. He must have known what their grandson was going to say but wasn't about to interrupt. Meanwhile, Orrin Lonetree whispered something to his wife, but she only shook her head. Sam cleared his throat once again, obviously wrestling with his announcement.

"All right." He made another attempt. "Ever since the, uh, accident, we've been thinking about how we could help you guys and show you how sorry we were."

Dylan's dad stiffened visibly, but Sam pressed on.

"We know maybe it's kind of weird when people you don't know take collections."

By this time, Dylan's dad was scratching his head and fidgeting, as if he was preparing to bolt or kick them all out of his house. This could get awkward in a hurry.

"Anyway, we just— We just—" Now Sam stalled for words, and he looked to his sister for help. She seemed ready to rescue him.

"We wanted to support our little brother," she said, "and Dylan too. So we went together and just wanted to add this to what he gave. It's not much, but—"

At this point Emily nodded at Sam, who pulled a bulging envelope from his pocket and extended it toward Dylan's parents as Emily finished her speech.

"But we really want you to have it, right, Sam?"

He nodded. "What she said."

At first the Lonetrees hesitated, and Charlotte could hardly watch as Brenda Lonetree looked at her husband, wiped a tear from her eye, and squeezed his arm.

"Please take it," said Emily. "You know the whole town is helping. There's collections at Mel's Place, Grandma's church-ladies group is doing a fundraiser. We're not the only ones."

"It's okay, Orrin," said Brenda, nudging her husband in the side. "Go ahead."

He cleared his throat and stepped away from Sam, clearly taken aback.

"I'm sorry." Sam started to set the envelope down on a chair next to the bed. "We didn't mean to put you on the spot. Maybe we should have—"

"No, I'm the one who's sorry." Orrin looked around the room. "I know you're just trying to help. You're good kids. Dylan has a good friend."

"We're just not used to this kind of thing," added Brenda, "that's all."

Her husband hesitated a moment longer before he finally reached out a shaking hand to accept the gift.

"She's right," he said, his voice uncertain. "We're not used to it, and I still don't understand why everybody is doing all this for us. But thank you."

Sam managed to say, "You're welcome," but it was clearly time to change the subject.

"For the pie!" added Dylan, holding up his blue cast in a victory salute.

The awkward moment ended with a round of laughter, for now, and Charlotte thought for a moment they were going to dig into the pie right there and then. Perhaps Dylan was getting hungry after only being able to eat Jell-O and chicken noodle soup.

"I'll have to send my husband out for more pie when

this is gone," said Dylan's mom, a broad smile on her face. "But what I want to know is, what would that say about my baking?"

They all laughed again, and Bob looked at Charlotte with their unspoken "time to go" signal, perfected over more than four decades of marriage. She understood his glance toward the door, and after a full round of good-byes and "Happy Thanksgivings," they finally left the room and made their way to the front door.

Brenda Lonetree caught up with Charlotte and Bob, her hands on their shoulders.

"I just wanted to tell you . . ." She bit her lip. "You must be very proud of those kids. Thank you again."

And then she turned away, leaving her husband to show them the door, and leaving Charlotte wondering exactly how much money Sam had handed over. But it was none of her business, and when they stepped outside Bob walked ahead when Christopher waved at him to hurry up. Only Pete hung back on the front walk with a soft tug at her coat sleeve.

"Mom," he kept his voice low. "Do you have any idea what the kids just did?"

She pressed her lips together and nodded, afraid that yes, she did. She watched them hurry on ahead toward the car.

"You don't think this is a sort of competitive thing, do you? Sibling rivalry?"

"I think it was just their way of sticking together." Pete pushed back the bill of his cap. "You know, one for all, all for one? They're really good at that kind of thing, you gotta admit. A lot more than me and Bill and Denise ever were."

True enough, though the comparison tugged at her heart. How could these grieving, unruly grandchildren have learned such a thing—something her own children had never really picked up? Perhaps in her effort to teach her grandchildren, they had taught her something even more profound.

"They emptied their pockets, Mom." Pete looked straight ahead when he told her. "Everything. I asked Sam about it last night when he insisted we come over here, and at first he wouldn't tell me, but I made him. Best I can tell, there was close to five hundred dollars in that envelope."

She caught her breath and glanced back at the house.

"So much?"

He nodded yes.

"So there goes his car fund, and she was going to buy a lot of stuff this Christmas too. You know they were saving up."

Charlotte didn't know what to think or say, though she almost felt guilty for knowing how much they had given—as if she had just pried into a very personal matter between the kids and God. And when they waved to her from the cars she picked up her pace.

"Come on, Grandma," Christopher called back. "We have one more surprise."

Chapter Twenty-Eight

By this time it was about ten in the morning, and Charlotte's panic had started to get the best of her. After all, on every other Thanksgiving she could remember, the turkey would be cooking by now, and all the fixings would be simmering in preparation for one of the biggest meals of the year.

But kidnapped in her own car, what could she do about it? And now none of the kids would answer her questions as they drove back through downtown Bedford in the direction of home, though they all seemed to share a secret.

"I take it we're not delivering the other pies," said Charlotte as they drove past Arleta's Cut-n-Curl Beauty Salon, then past the dark windows and the "May your heart never be CLOSED to Jesus" sign hanging in the glass door of Mel's Place.

The kids just smiled and didn't answer as they continued out of town and eventually turned onto Heather Creek Road toward home. Apparently they had no other stops, which was a small comfort. In time Christopher bounced in his seat, craned his neck, and looked out ahead as they turned back up the driveway.

"Keep your belt on," warned Sam, but he couldn't keep the cap on Christopher's bottled enthusiasm.

"You're going to like this, Grandma," Christopher bubbled. "You're really going to like this."

She spotted Melody's small blue pickup parked next to the house.

"She must be here for the pies," Charlotte said as they pulled to a stop. But by the time they'd all climbed out of the car and trooped inside the kitchen, it was clear something else was going on.

"So there you are! Welcome!" Melody looked up with a smile from stirring a pot of simmering gravy. With her stained professional apron and hair pulled back in a pony tail, it looked for all the world as if Charlotte had just stepped into *her* kitchen, instead of the other way around. Finally, Charlotte just had to grab the nearest hostage by the arm and hold on.

"All right," she said in mock seriousness, "I'm not letting Christopher go until somebody tells me exactly what's going on here."

"Don't you see?" Melody beamed as she spread her arms wide, dripping gravy on the stove. "You've been doing for everybody else, nonstop. I've been running you ragged with all this pie stuff. Now it's my turn to, well, I'm just helping you out with dinner today, that's all. You deserve it."

That's when Charlotte noticed Ashley in the dining room, busily setting the table that had been covered with a gold-and-brown-checked harvest tablecloth. Ashley waved at Emily and then looked away when Sam walked into the room. Charlotte thought she detected the faintest hint of red in her cheeks. She let Christopher loose when she saw elegant white candles glowing everywhere from festive table decorations of yellow gourds and dried cornhusks.

Oh, and the smells! Charlotte breathed deeply the aroma of roasting turkey, of rolls and gravy, of tart cranberries . . . How had Melody managed it all, and so quickly?

"I brought a few things from the restaurant." Melody shrugged as if she had guessed Charlotte's question. "I just hope you don't mind relaxing this year while someone else cooks. If you do mind, that's too bad."

"Well." Charlotte was pretty sure she wouldn't be joining the boys in front of a televised football game, and she glanced around her kitchen, wondering how to respond. Toby interrupted with loud barking from just outside the door.

"Oh, and one other thing," said Melody. "Bob insisted, actually. Russ and Will should be coming too. Maybe that's them."

Actually it was Bob's sister Rosemary, who greeted everyone with hugs and a big smile as she stepped inside. She was followed not long after that by Melody's stocky husband Russ, along with fifteen-year-old son Brett, gangly and shy. Even as the others stepped through the kitchen though, Pete peered out the window at a small red car bouncing its way down the driveway.

"Are we expecting anyone else?" asked Charlotte. Melody shook her head.

"Not that I know of."

Pete knew who it was though, and a minute later opened

the door to welcome Dana Simons, flushed and holding a soggy paper grocery sack out in front of her.

"Happy Thanksgiving!" Dana announced from the top step. "My grandmother made her famous cinnamon rolls and said I should drop some by. We know how busy it's been for you, and—"

"Goodness!" Melody still had full control of the situation. "Don't stand there letting all the cold air in. Bring that girl inside, Pete!"

"No, it's a family time for you." Dana hesitated. "I really couldn't—"

"Nonsense!" Charlotte took her by the hand. "You're very welcome here. Please. Unless you have other plans?"

By then Dana must have caught sight of some of the other people inside, and not just family.

"Well, maybe just for a little while."

"And let me see those cinnamon rolls," boomed Melody. She proceeded to direct traffic with her gravy spoon and presided over both the oven and stove. For the next couple of hours she even allowed Charlotte and Ashley to help, though for the most part she just pushed them out of the kitchen loaded up with trays full of snacks.

By now the house had filled to the rafters with the sound of people and laughter, just the way Charlotte liked it. The only ones missing would be Bill and Anna and the girls, since this year was their turn to spend Thanksgiving with Anna's folks in Omaha.

"So everyone knew about this but me?" Charlotte finally asked Melody, back in the kitchen. "You nearly drove me to a nervous breakdown, Melody Givens. Whatever happened to the poor woman who wanted the pies for her dying mother. You didn't make that up, did you, just to get me out of the house for the morning?"

"Oh no, dear." Melody put up her hand, as if she was in court. "Every word I told you was true. They really said they were coming for the pies."

"The truth?"

Melody raised both hands, acting miffed that Charlotte would even question her.

"I even gave them directions to your place—although if they're not here by now, I'm starting to wonder if they got lost or the weather slowed them down. Anyway, I have to admit it worked out as a handy excuse to get you out of here today."

"*Hmm.* I still think it was a bit underhanded."

"Not at all. Now go sit down, please. We're almost ready to eat."

Once again, Charlotte had no choice. After they'd all been seated, Melody brought out plates of mashed potatoes and sweet potatoes, fancy china tureens swimming with savory dark gravy, Melody's secret-recipe stuffing with sliced sausages and celery, mountains of golden brown rolls accompanied by butter and jam, bowls brimming with bright green peas and two kinds of cranberries—not to mention several large platters of sliced turkey, each featuring both light meat and dark. There was even a vegetarian tofu "turkey" roast for Emily.

While everyone else oohed and ahhed at the incoming spread, Christopher quickly reached for one of the drumsticks with his hands. But Emily gave him an even quicker warning slap.

"What do you think the serving fork is for, huh?"

Well, Charlotte might have put it more delicately, but she didn't mind that the point was made. Christopher protested but dutifully reached for the proper utensil.

"Actually, er—" Bob pinged on the side of a bottle of sparkling cider and got to his feet. "Maybe I'd better offer a word of thanks before we dig in. To Melody, and to the Lord."

Melody wiped her hands on a dishrag and waved them off with a smile.

"I know this is a little different," she told them. "I'm just glad you're all flexible. Not that anyone asked *you,* Charlotte."

Charlotte looked around at her gathered family and friends, at the long table piled high with wonderful food. Right now she wasn't going to be giving any speeches, or she might break down. Today she would leave that to the others.

Emily flipped the bill of Sam's baseball cap so he would take it off, and they all finally bowed together.

"Heavenly Father," Bob began, his voice low, "we are grateful for these, thy gifts. We're thankful thou hast brought us together, and for teaching us something new. Putting others before ourselves, for example. And accepting gifts from others. I also thank thee for a family who is willing to take over Heather Creek Farm and keep it going for at least another generation. Or maybe two, if we can get my younger son married off soon enough."

Pete snorted and Charlotte peeked over to see Dana's face turning red, but Bob continued with his prayer.

"But most of all, Lord, we thank thee for the lessons in

pies, and for thy tender mercies this Thanksgiving, for we pray in the name of our Savior, amen."

They had hardly opened their eyes and lifted their heads when Christopher piped up.

"Does that mean you're not selling the farm, after all?"

Pete and Bob exchanged an amused glance while Bob turned a little pale.

"Selling the farm?" asked Bob, shaking his head. "Why would we do that?"

Pete reached over to muss Christopher's hair.

"No chance, dude. I don't know where you got that idea, but we're not going anywhere. Guaranteed."

That seemed to satisfy Christopher. He whooped and clapped as Charlotte passed him a plate of peas. Right now though, Charlotte simply enjoyed the feast, as Melody had ordered her to do. Everything tasted so much better because she had not cooked any of it with her own hands. Melody hovered over them, pouring sparkling cider, swapping empty baskets with ones full of steaming rolls, even scurrying out with reheated gravy for seconds.

"Melody," Charlotte told her friend, "you shouldn't have gone to all this trouble."

"Too late." Melody added more chunky cranberry sauce to the table. "And besides, you need to keep showing these kids how to be a gracious receiver."

Christopher must have overheard. He was working on his second helping of turkey with a generous extra helping of gravy and yet another fluffy dinner roll laden with sweet raspberry jam.

"Like in football?" he asked, and Charlotte didn't understand the connection at first.

"You know, a wide receiver?"

This only brought groans from Ashley, Emily, and Sam, who were finishing up their own plates.

Charlotte had to laugh as she held up her own glass to propose a toast while the rest of the family paused from cleaning up their plates.

"To my baking helpers," she said. "And to Melody, who made this wonderful meal possible. We're *all* thankful."

"Oh, but it's not over yet," announced Melody, balancing several plates on her way back to the kitchen. "We've got pumpkin, cherry-berry, and apple-caramel. I've heard they're the best in Nebraska." Melody winked at Charlotte.

Emily caught the giggles first, and when she looked at Ashley it only got worse. Soon Sam and Christopher joined in, Rosemary and Dana too. Finally Bob and Pete added their deep belly laughs as Melody brought in cinnamon rolls and coffee.

After everyone had eaten their fill and more, Melody and Ashley cleared dishes while the men loosened their belts. Charlotte had to hold herself back from jumping up to help.

"Are you sure you don't want me to do something?" she asked Melody. "It feels as if I ought to be, you know."

"You would offend me if you did, dear." Melody patted her on the arm as she whisked by. "Now please just relax and have another roll, would you?"

"I'm relaxing." Christopher moaned and leaned back in

his chair, pushing aside his plate. "I just wish I had room for one more course."

"Actually," said Uncle Pete, "there *is* one more."

They all looked toward the kitchen. Surely Melody didn't have more food on the way.

"You're kidding, right?" asked Sam. "Can we, like, save it for later on tonight? Or maybe tomorrow even? I'm so totally stuffed I can't even think of another bite."

"Nope." Pete stood and pushed out his chair. "The final course is for now, and it's outside."

"Why am I not surprised that you can't wait?" asked Charlotte. She followed Pete with the rest of them, out through the back door.

"Are we going to need our jackets for this?" asked Ashley, shivering in the cold. She had obviously not been let in on the secret either. Uncle Pete didn't hear her question though, so she shrugged and followed the crowd outside.

"So what's the surprise?" asked Sam, stomping his feet and rubbing his arms to keep warm. His words rose in a cloud of frost. Pete just grinned and fished a set of keys out of his pocket and then tossed them to Sam. He motioned with his head toward the barn.

"Just inside the doors," said Pete. "It's yours."

Sam looked from Pete to the barn and wrinkled his forehead in confusion. "Huh?"

"Unless you don't want it." Pete shrugged. "Go on. Take a look."

By this time Christopher had run over to the barn doors and started tugging them open.

"Hey!" Sam objected. "Wait just a minute."

Christopher hung on and swung himself out—revealing a dusty, tarp-covered vehicle just inside. Sam looked more confused than ever.

"Pull off the tarp!" Pete told him. Sam and Christopher wasted no time, revealing a rather road-worn little car that had probably once looked quite sporty.

"Did you say *mine*?" Sam fumbled for the right words. "But how did you—"

"I got it in a trade a few weeks back from a guy here in town who needed a little work on his house. Didn't know what to do with it at the time, so I just stuck it in here. But after, you know, all that with the Dylan kid . . ." Pete's voice trailed off. "Course, I could always just fix it and sell it for a couple hundred bucks if you don't want it."

"No way! Wait! You're kidding, right?" Sam ran his hand over the curved top of the car. Judging by the multiple colors, it had been painted several times over the years, but the curved, low-slung look gave it a sort of sports car pedigree. "This is a 240-Z. A total classic!"

"Well, yeah." Pete laughed. "But it's a seventy-two, so it might need some work."

Sam's mouth still hung wide open.

"This is an early Christmas present. Dessert first, I always say."

Sam looked at Charlotte and Bob as if looking for their approval. What else could Charlotte do but smile and nod?

"As long as you always give your brother and sister a ride when they need one," she told him. "And no speeding!"

Luckily, the little car didn't look like it would move very quickly anyway, despite its sporty styling. She glanced at Bob with a questioning glance.

"You knew about this?" she whispered. Bob shrugged as if he had no idea, but that only meant he did. And Pete looked as excited to give this gift as Sam looked at receiving it.

"I really did get a deal on this thing," Pete told them as they watched the kids eagerly slip inside the little two-door. "I think it's been sitting in the guy's garage for the past fifteen years collecting dust."

"Start it up!" Bob encouraged him.

And Sam did try, in between his repeated thank yous and variations of "I can't believe this!"

But after a couple of cold cranks, the car would only make a discouraging clicking sound every time Sam turned the key. He rolled down the window.

"Actually . . ." Pete walked around to the driver's side and leaned in. "He said it probably needed a new battery. Guess I should have listened."

"So what now?" Sam wondered, but even Charlotte knew the answer to this one. She walked over to the back end and gave it a little nudge with her knee.

"What's the matter?" she asked. "Haven't you ever push-started a car before?"

Well, this teenager still had a thing or two to learn, even about cars. For now she, Bob, Pete, and Dana lined up behind it while Rosemary stood off to the side, and Pete took charge.

"Let us get it up to speed," she said. "Keep the clutch in, put it in first gear, and then pop the clutch when I yell. Got it?"

Sam gave a thumbs-up, and fortunately the little car moved along easily, even on the gravel drive. Toby hobbled alongside as best she could.

"Not much to it, huh?" Pete grunted as they got the car rolling faster and faster. Gravel crunched under bald tires as they pushed. "Easier than push-starting the old truck."

"Now!" yelled Charlotte.

With a jerk and a sputter Sam succeeded in starting his new car, pumping the gas so it roared to life. Between gasps for air, they all cheered and clapped while Sam honked the horn and headed down the driveway. A little jerky, to be sure, and the muffler sounded horribly loud, but it did run.

Perhaps, thought Charlotte, *Sam's new car is going to need a bit more than just a new battery.*

But Emily waved out the window, almost as excited as her brother.

"Oh, wait a minute!" Pete came to life and ran after them down the driveway, waving his arms. "There's presents in the back end for Emily and Christopher too. Wait, you guys! Hold on!"

Charlotte had to laugh softly at the comical scene: the new old little sports car limping down the gravel way and the uncle, limping along behind them. She wondered what he had come up with for the other two, though she guessed it might not take much to match the value of the old car.

"There they go," said Bob, chuckling and leaning on his

knees as he caught his breath. Charlotte draped an arm around his shoulders as they watched their grandchildren pause at Heather Creek Road with a loud backfire. Pete could only watch them disappear as well, and he skidded to a stop. Good thing there wasn't any traffic this time of day.

"So did we train them up the way they should go?" Charlotte wondered aloud as Bob straightened up. He gave her a warm kiss on the cheek as they steered back toward the warmth of their kitchen.

"They're not quite out the door yet, woman. We still have a little time left to work on this project of ours."

She smiled. Well, yes. Perhaps they did.

Charlotte's Apple-Caramel Pie

1 pastry crust for a deep-dish nine- or
ten-inch pie (see recipe below)

½ cup sugar
3½ tablespoons all-purpose flour
1 teaspoon cinnamon
⅛ teaspoon salt
6–7 cups thinly sliced peeled apples
(Fuji or Granny Smith)
1 tablespoon lemon juice
1 recipe for the crumb topping
(see recipe below)

⅓–½ cup chopped pecans (optional)
¼ cup caramel sundae topping

In a large bowl, stir together the sugar, flour, cinnamon, and salt. Add the apple slices and lemon juice, and gently toss until coated. Transfer apple mixture to the prepared pie shell and sprinkle the crumb topping over apple mixture.

Bake in a preheated 375-degree oven for sixty to sixty-five minutes. After thirty minutes, rotate the pie for even baking. Remove from the oven when apple mixture is bubbly. Top with the chopped pecans and drizzle with the caramel topping. Cool on a wire rack. Serve warm with ice cream.

Perfect Pie Pastry Crust

2 cups all-purpose flour
1 teaspoon salt
⅔ cup plus 2 tablespoons shortening
5–6 tablespoons ice water

Mix flour and salt in a medium bowl. Cut in shortening until particles are the size of small peas (don't overwork). Sprinkle with ice water and toss with a fork lightly until all flour is moistened. (One to two teaspoons more water may be added if needed.)

Coat hands lightly with flour, and gather pastry into a ball. Shape into a flattened round on a lightly floured surface. Handle as little as possible. Roll pastry using a floured rolling pin into a circle two to three inches larger than the upside-down pie plate. Place the rolled pastry into the pie plate. Leave enough pastry to fold over and flute the edges as desired, and trim off the excess.

Crumb Topping

¾ cup packed brown sugar
½ teaspoon cinnamon
½ cup all-purpose flour
½ cup quick-cooking rolled oats
½ cup cold butter

Stir together brown sugar, cinnamon, flour, and rolled oats. Cut in the butter until topping is like coarse crumbs.

About the Author

Robert Elmer is a former pastor and small-town newspaper editor who began writing novels during evenings and weekends, often after the rest of the family was asleep. Today he has written more than fifty books for youths and adults, including *The Duet, The Celebrity, The Recital,* and *Like Always*. He enjoys speaking at schools, serves on the editorial board of the Jerry B. Jenkins Christian Writers Guild, and lives with his wife, Ronda, near a beautiful lake in rural Idaho. Find out more at www.RobertElmerBooks.com.

A Note from the Editors

This original book was created by the Books and Inspirational Media Division of Guideposts, the world's leading inspirational publisher. Founded in 1945 by Dr. Norman Vincent Peale and Ruth Stafford Peale, Guideposts helps people from all walks of life achieve their maximum personal and spiritual potential. Guideposts is committed to communicating positive, faith-filled principles for people everywhere to use in successful daily living.

Our publications include award-winning magazines such as *Guideposts* and *Angels on Earth*, best-selling books, and outreach services that demonstrate what can happen when faith and positive thinking are applied in day-to-day life.

For more information, visit us at www.guideposts.com, call (800) 431-2344 or write Guideposts, PO Box 5815, Harlan, Iowa 51593.